"Thank you for dinner." Bree leaned in, one hand pressed to his chest, and kissed him on the cheek. Her soft scent and body heat surrounded him.

He hadn't expected the innocent kiss or that he'd be overwhelmed by her nearness.

Bree's mouth lingered near his as she pulled away slowly. So slow he could hear every microsecond ticking in his head as he tried to catch his breath. He willed himself to stay in control, to keep his hands shoved in his pockets where they wouldn't get him into trouble.

"You're welcome." The words came out much quieter than he'd intended. He dropped his gaze to her sensual lips and she smiled.

"I'd ask you in for an after-dinner drink, but like you said, we've got an early morning." Her voice was soft and captivating, an unspoken invitation.

Wes wet his lower lip and tried to tear his attention away from her mouth and her soft gaze. Tried with every fiber of his being to ignore the fact that he wanted her desperately.

He couldn't.

Dear Reader,

I've always been enchanted with fiction's ability to transport us to faraway places and acquaint us with unfamiliar experiences.

In *Playing with Seduction*, UK event promoter Wesley Adams returns to his native North Carolina to establish his business stateside. He and Brianna Evans, the reigning queen of American beach volleyball, take a road trip to get reacquainted with the state. As you accompany them to iconic locations in Raleigh and Asheville, you'll want to pack your bags and venture there to experience each location for yourself.

You'll also take an emotional journey with this couple as each of them struggles with the past in a way that threatens to derail their future together.

Enjoy your adventure with Wesley and Brianna. Then, for series news, reader giveaways and more, join my VIP Readers list at reeseryan.com.

Happy reading,

Reese Ryan

Playing
WITH
Seduction

REESE RYAN

HARLEQUIN® KIMANI™ ROMANCE

Recycling programs
for this product may
not exist in your area.

ISBN-13: 978-1-335-21650-2

Playing with Seduction

Copyright © 2018 by Roxanne Ravenel

HARLEQUIN®
TM www.Harlequin.com

Printed in U.S.A.

Reese Ryan is a multi-published author of romantic fiction featuring complex and deliciously flawed characters. She challenges her heroines with family and career drama, reformed bad boys, and life-changing secrets while treating readers to an emotional love story and unexpected twists.

Past president of her local Romance Writers of America chapter and a panelist at the 2017 *Los Angeles Times* Festival of Books, Reese is an advocate for the romance genre and diversity in fiction.

A native of The Land (Cleveland, OH), Reese resides in North Carolina where she carefully treads the line between being a Southerner and a Yankee, despite her insistence on calling soda *pop*. She gauges her progress by the number of "bless your lil' hearts" she receives each week. She is currently down to two.

Connect with Reese via Instagram, Facebook or reeseryan.com.

Books by Reese Ryan

Harlequin Kimani Romance

Dedicated to all the remarkable readers I've met during my publishing journey. You support African American and multicultural romance with your hard-earned dollars, valuable time, honest reviews and enthusiastic word of mouth. We are nothing without you.

Acknowledgments

Thank you, Shannon Criss and Keyla Hernandez, for believing in me and acquiring *Playing with Desire*— the first book in my Pleasure Cove series.

I am truly grateful for your enthusiastic support of my career and your role in affording me other opportunities within Harlequin.

It has truly been a pleasure to work with you both. And it has been an honor to join the ranks of the remarkable Kimani Romance authors I have long admired.

Chapter 1

The click of high heels against the hardwood floors prompted Wesley Adams to look up from his magazine.

A mature, attractive blonde extended her hand, her coral lips pressed into a wide smile. "Pleasure to meet you, Mr. Adams. I'm Miranda Hopkins, executive director of Westbrook Charitable Foundation."

"The pleasure is mine." Wes stood and shook her hand. "But please, call me Wes."

"Wes, I'm sorry to tell you Liam won't be joining us for today's meeting." Miranda frowned. "One of the girls isn't feeling well, so he stayed home with her."

"No, I wasn't aware." Wes was surprised his best friend hadn't called him. After all, Liam had hounded him for more than a month to fly in from London for this meeting in Pleasure Cove. The woman looked worried he'd bolt, so Wes forced a smile. "But I'm confident he left me in good hands."

"You've managed some impressive events in the UK," Miranda said in her heavy, Southern drawl as she guided him toward a carpeted hallway. "We're so excited that you're considering taking on our project."

Wes nodded and thanked her, glad his friend had clearly gotten the point. He was here to assess the project and decide whether it was a good fit. Nothing was written in stone.

As they approached an open door of a glass-walled conference room, he heard the voices of two women. One of them was oddly familiar.

"Wes, this is our events manager, Lisa Chastain." He reached out to shake Lisa's hand. Then Miranda drew his attention to the other woman. "And this is Olympic champion and international beach-volleyball star Brianna Evans. Bree, this is Wesley—"

"Adams. We've met." Her expression soured, as if she smelled a rotting corpse. It sure as hell wasn't her glad-to-see-you-again-Wes face.

Bloody hell.

He hadn't seen Bree since the night they met at that little club in London's West End more than a year ago.

Liam, I'm going to strangle you.

He'd tell his friend what he thought of his matchmaking attempt later. For now, he'd play it cool. After all, he hadn't done anything wrong. But Bree, whose lips were pursed as she stared at him through narrow slits, obviously disagreed.

Wes widened the smile he'd honed while attending boarding school with kids whose parents made more in a month than his parents made all year. He extended his hand to Bree, despite the look on her face that dared him to touch her.

Bree shoved a limp hand into his, then withdrew it quickly, as if her palm was on fire.

What did, or didn't, happen between he and Bree was personal. *This* was business.

"I believe Miss Evans has a bone to pick with me." Wes pulled out Brianna's chair and gestured for her to have a seat.

She narrowed her gaze at him, then took her seat. As she turned toward the two women, who exchanged worried glances, Bree forced a laugh. "Wes predicted my alma mater wouldn't make it back to the Sweet Sixteen, and he was right. I'm convinced he jinxed us."

Nicely done.

Wes acknowledged her save with a slight nod. He slipped into the chair across from her—the only open seat with an information packet placed on it.

The night they'd met in London, her eyes, flecked with gold, had gazed dreamily into his. The coy, flirtatious vibe she exuded that night was gone.

Bree's face dripped with disdain. Anger vibrated off her smooth, brown skin—the color of a bar of milk chocolate melting in the hot summer sun.

Wes only realized he'd been staring at Bree when she cleared her throat and opened her information packet.

"Well, I…" Miranda's gaze darted between Brianna and Wes. "We're all here. Let's get started, shall we?"

The meeting was quick and efficient. Miranda and Lisa were respectful of their time and promised they would be throughout the course of planning and executing a celebrity volleyball tournament over the next six months.

Six entire months.

Liam had laid out a dream project for him. The perfect vehicle for expanding his successful UK event planning and promotions company to the US. However, working with Bree Evans for six months would be as pleasant as having an appendectomy, followed by a root canal. On repeat.

The meeting concluded with a full tour of the expansive Pleasure Cove Luxury Resort property. After they toured the main building, the four of them loaded into a golf cart. Wes slipped into the backseat beside Bree and tried not to notice how the smooth, brown skin on her long legs glistened. But her attempts to keep her leg from touching his only drew his attention.

The Westbrooks had gone all-out with the property. In addition to the main building there were four other buildings on either side of it that housed guests. There was a pool and spa house, four different restaurants, a poolside grill, tennis courts and two workout facilities. Large rental homes and a building with smaller, connected guest houses completed the vast property.

"Here we are at the guest houses, where you'll both be staying. Your luggage has already been taken to your individual guest houses," Miranda announced. "Wes you're in guest house five and Bree, I believe you're right next door in guest house six."

Of course.

"Makes it convenient to chat about the project whenever you'd like." Lisa grinned.

"It certainly does." Wes loosened his tie and stepped out of the golf cart. He extended a hand to

Bree, but she stepped out of her side of the cart and walked around.

"See you at the next meeting. If you want to knock around some ideas before then, just give me a call," Miranda said. She and Lisa waved goodbye as they zipped off in the golf cart.

Wes took a deep breath before he turned to Bree. "Look, I'm sorry I didn't call—"

"You're an ass." She shifted the strap of her purse higher.

She wasn't wrong.

Still, the accusation felt like a ton of bricks being launched onto his chest. "Bree, you're obviously angry—"

"Don't call me Bree. We're not friends." She folded her arms over her breasts, dragging his gaze there.

Wes raised his eyes to hers again. "Okay, what should I call you?"

Psycho? Insane? Ridiculously hot in that tight little black dress?

The corner of her mouth quirked in a grin that was gone almost as quickly as it had appeared. She'd caught him staring and seemed to relish his reaction. "Call me Brianna or Ms. Evans. I don't really care." Though, clearly, she did.

"All right, Ms. Evans." *Ms. Jackson, if you're nasty.* He bit his lip, scrubbing the image from his brain of her moving her hips and striking a pose. "I'd like to sincerely apologize for not calling when I said I would. It was rude of me. I should've called."

"You shouldn't have promised." Her voice was shaky for a moment. "Don't promise something if you don't intend to carry it out. That's one of the basic rules of not being an ass hat."

"Noted." He chuckled as he pulled his shades from his inside jacket pocket and put them on. "We good?"

"As good as we need to be." Brianna turned on her tall heels, which added length to her mile-long legs. His gaze followed the sway of her generous hips. She opened the door of her guest house and glanced over her shoulder momentarily before stepping inside and closing the door behind her.

Wesley sighed. He'd spent more than a decade building his event-planning-and-promotion business from a ragtag team of university misfits planning pop-up events for a little extra dosh to a company that routinely planned events for some of the hottest celebs and largest corporations in the UK. Taking point on the planning of the Westbrook's new celebrity volleyball tournament would help him establish a name with major players in the US more quickly.

But would Bree's animosity make it impossible for them to work together effectively?

He'd lived in London the better part of his life, and he loved living there. Still, the blue skies, warm sun and salty breeze drifting in from the Atlantic Ocean made him nostalgic for home.

But then he hadn't really gone home. He hadn't even told his mother he was in North Carolina.

Maybe he only missed the idea of home.

Either way, it was time to find out.

Bree tossed her purse onto the nearest chair and flopped down onto the sandy beige sofa. It was the same color as Wesley's pants. Not that she cared. She just happened to notice the color, and how well the material had hugged his firm bottom.

No. No. No. Do not think about his ass or any other parts of his anatomy.

She kicked off her shoes and headed to the bar. It was well-stocked, courtesy of Liam Westbrook. But she also had Liam to thank for bringing her and Wes together on this project.

The stunned look on Wes's face indicated that he was just as surprised to see her. Liam obviously hadn't told his friend that he'd invited her to work on the project.

But why?

They were best friends. Which meant Liam probably knew what had happened that night.

Her cheeks stung as she surveyed the bottles of wine. *No.* It was too early to drink chardonnay alone. She pulled out a split of champagne and a bottle of orange juice.

It's never too early for mimosas.

She took a sip of the cocktail and felt she could breathe for the first time since she'd laid eyes on Wesley Adams. His six-foot-three frame had filled out the navy jacket and beige pants as if they were made for him.

Bree checked the time on her phone. It was still early out in California. After a recent shoulder surgery, her best friend and volleyball partner, Rebecca Jacobs wouldn't be following her usual early morning workout routine. Still, it wouldn't hurt to text.

Bree sent a text message with one hand while nursing her drink in the other. Bex, you up?

Within seconds Bex replied. Uh-oh. How'd your meeting go?

Bree sighed. Was she really that transparent? Then again, she and Bex had been partners for the last seven years, so there wasn't much she could put past her friend. Meeting was great. Unfortunately, I would have to work with the devil himself. Don't know if I can do this.

The phone rang within seconds of her sending the text.

"What the hell is going on?"

Bree laughed. "Good morning to you, too."

"Sorry. Good morning. Now, what the hell is going on? Who was at the meeting that would make you want to pass up this opportunity?"

She sighed, her finger tracing the bar. "Wes Adams."

"The guy you met at the bar that night in London?" Bex let out a sigh of relief. "I know you're bummed he didn't call, but he's a guy. Don't take it personally. In fact, you should be glad you guys didn't sleep together. That'd be awkward."

"Today was awkward." Bree balanced the phone between her ear and shoulder as she wrestled with the plastic-wrapped gift basket filled with goodies. She could use some chocolate. Stat.

"Why? Because you guys fooled around a little? You are seriously out of practice, my friend." She laughed. "I told you not having a life would catch up with you."

"Volleyball *is* my life." Bree ripped open a chocolate truffle and stuffed it in her mouth.

"And it's a great life, but it won't always be there.

We're approaching thirty. Time to start thinking about life after volleyball."

"You aren't thinking of retiring on me, are you?" Bree mumbled through a mouthful of chocolate.

"No, but this injury has given me a lot of time to think. I don't want to wake up one day and feel like I missed out on the things that are really important."

"Like?" Her friend was surprisingly philosophical. It made Bree uneasy. She was usually the one reminding Bex to be more frugal and save for the future, when tournament money, appearance fees and endorsements were no longer flowing in, something they'd both been forced to think about more lately.

"I dunno. Like a husband. Maybe kids."

"Wow." Bree's mouth curled in a smirk. "So what's his name?"

"Shut up." Bex fell suspiciously quiet before releasing a long sigh. "His name is Nick. He's my physical therapist, and he is so cute."

"Uh-huh."

"But we're not talking about me right now, Bree. This is about you. Why is running in to this guy again such a big deal? Do you have a serious thing for him or something?"

"No." Even to her ears, her response sounded like that of a tween in denial, punctuated by an unladylike snort. Her mother would be so proud.

Bex paused, which told Bree that she heard her unconvincing denial, but chose to ignore it. "Then no harm, no foul. Certainly nothing worth giving up this opportunity. You could become the face of the hottest new beach volleyball event on the East Coast. Besides, Westbrook International Luxury Resorts is

a worldwide organization. This could be the beginning of spreading your brand. *Our* brand. So don't
wuss out on me."

Bree gritted her teeth and stared out onto the water.
A huge wave licked the shore, the chilly waters chas-
ing away a toy Pomeranian. "Okay, fine. I'll figure
out how to deal with it. With him."

"That a girl. Whatever it takes. Just like on the
court. Got it?"

Bree chucked the truffle she was about to open
back into its box and nodded. "Got it. Whatever it
takes."

She talked to Bex for another half hour, getting
an update on her injured shoulder and her hot new
physical therapist before finally ending the call. Bree
changed into a pair of yoga pants, a T-shirt and a
sweater. She stepped out onto the back deck and inhaled the salty ocean breeze. It was sixty-two degrees
out. A fairly warm day for early February.

She flopped onto the chaise and tried to remember
her friend's words. They hadn't slept together. So why
was she still so pissed at him?

Because she'd wanted to sleep with him. God, she'd
wanted to. She'd fantasized about it in the wee hours
of the morning, when she couldn't shake the memory
of his kiss from her brain.

She shuddered, remembering the touch of his hand
when she'd been all but obligated to shake it and make
up that story about why she was upset with him. There
was some truth to the story.

A slight smile played on Bree's lips as she remembered their argument about what football team had a
chance of winning the Super Bowl. She just left out the

part where he'd asked her to come back to his place.
Bree had turned him down. He smiled, his eyes filled
with understanding. Then he gave her the sweetest
kiss. Sweet and innocent, yet filled with the promise
of passionate nights ahead. They'd only spent a few
hours together, but he'd managed to make the kiss feel
meaningful. Real.

Real enough that she'd stared at her phone for a
week afterward, waiting for him to call. Like he'd
promised after their kiss.

Her response that night kept replaying in her head.
Sorry, but I'm not that kind of girl. She laughed bit-
terly. True, she wasn't the kind of girl who normally
believed in one-night stands. In fact, she wasn't the
kind of girl who got laid at all. Not for a very long
time. Not since…

She tried to erase the memory of the scornful
mouth and hard, dark eyes she'd once found so in-
triguing. Sexy even. She'd been wrong about that
asshole. Apparently, she'd been just as wrong about
Wesley Adams.

The man was handsome and tall with warm brown
skin. An athletic body that had felt incredible pressed
against hers on the dance floor. And a killer smile.
One worthy of a toothpaste commercial. He had the
straightest, most brilliant teeth she'd ever seen.

And she loved his laugh, which he employed often.
Because he was funny. And smart. And he liked
sports. Just like she did. But he wasn't intimidated
because she was knowledgeable about sports and full
of opinions she readily shared. He was the kind of
guy she could see herself spending time with on those

lonely nights she actually got to spend in her own bed back in Huntington Beach.

Wes was the kind of guy she wanted to spend more than one night with, so she'd turned down his offer to go back to his place.

She'd gone to the pub with Bex that night, determined to crawl out of all the insecurities that rumbled around in her head, barely leaving elbow room for her own thoughts.

She went to The Alley that night, intending to take someone back to her hotel. Just once she wanted to be a little naughty. To shed the good-girl image she'd worked so hard to perfect over the past two decades.

She was the scholarship kid who struggled to fit in at a private school, terrified that the kids would find out she lived in the run-down projects. Two of the front stairs missing and not a single blade of grass on their "lawn."

She'd spent the past ten years creating her image as the perfect spokesperson. A successful player with a feel-good story and the kind of good-girl image that garnered endorsements and kept them. Not the kind of girl who would stroll into a club and pick up a random guy for the night.

In the end, she hadn't turned him down to protect her shiny, good-girl reputation. She politely turned down his offer because she liked him.

Really liked him.

So she gambled on there being another night between them. Only there wasn't. Bree was angry at Wes for not keeping his promise. She was angry with herself for not taking him up on his offer.

Bree drew her legs against her chest, wrapping her

arms around them. If she was going to be working with Wes Adams for the next six months, she'd have to start thinking with her brain, not her libido. And she couldn't behave like a jilted lover.

Her heart fluttered, just thinking about how her hand felt in his, even for a moment. A glowing warmth arose through her fingers, making its way to her chest.

She put her head on her knees and sighed.

Letting go of her silly crush on Wes would be easier said than done.

Chapter 2

Wes rang Liam's cell four times.

No answer.

His best friend was definitely dodging him. It was probably best. He had a few choice words for Liam. No way it had just slipped his mind to mention that he'd selected Bree Evans to work on this project, too.

Not that Bree wasn't the ideal person to front an annual sports-and-music festival with the potential to be a huge draw for the resort. She was.

Bree was one of the top beach volleyball players in the world. One of the few players of color to gain endorsements and a huge following. She was genuinely nice. Frequently participated in charity events. And the camera loved her.

Every single inch of her. A gorgeous smile. A curvy frame anchored by her voluptuous breasts and an ass that would give any red-blooded man reason to adjust his trousers. Long legs. Strong, lean thighs. Undulating hips.

Wes scrubbed a hand down his face. Sitting there recounting the finer points of Bree's physique wasn't a productive use of his time, or a very good way to maintain his sanity. He glanced over at the wall that separated their units. Tried not to wonder what she was doing. If she'd slipped out of the thigh-hugging black dress she wore at the meeting.

He'd like to think she'd worn it for him. The surprise on her lovely face meant she clearly hadn't. Wes shook his head and sighed. Liam couldn't dodge him forever. In the meantime, he had business of his own to handle.

Wes grabbed the key to the loaner car Liam left for him and headed to the front door. Time to go home.

The gravel crunched in the driveway of the old bungalow his grandmother once owned. His mother had left England five years ago and returned to North Carolina to take care of his grandmother, who had taken a tumble down the narrow stairs and broken a hip. After his grandmother passed, his mother decided to stay in her childhood home. A home that held lots of memories for him, too.

Wes stepped out of the red Dodge Challenger with black leather. The loaner was another enticement from Liam to take on the project. Perhaps also an apology before the fact for springing Bree Evans on him without warning. He shut the door and headed up the driveway. There was no answer, so he knocked. Twice.

Finally he heard footsteps inside and the turning of

locks. The door swung open, releasing a dark, musty odor that made him wonder if he'd arrived at the wrong house.

"Wes? Baby, what are you doing here?" Lena Adams looked tired and slightly haggard. She ran her hand down the soiled apron she was wearing and smiled, then pushed open the screen door. "It's so good to see you."

He wrapped his long arms around his mother, her face buried in his chest. "Good to see you, too, Mom." His gaze traveled around the room. A thick layer of dust had settled on the furniture. Dust bunnies inhabited the corners. Stacks of books and papers were piled on various surfaces around the living room and dining room. If he wasn't holding his mother in his arms now, he wouldn't have believed he was in her house.

Lena had been the house manager for a wealthy family for two decades. She'd administered weekly white-glove tests, making her the bane of the housekeepers' existence. She would settle for nothing less than absolute cleanliness. Which led to much of her frustration with him, as a boy. Even while caring for his grandmother, she'd managed to keep the place immaculate.

What's going on?

His mother finally released him. She squeezed his hands in hers. "I can't believe you didn't tell me you were coming. I would've gotten the place ready and invited your brother up from Atlanta for a few days." She looked behind him. "Where are your bags?"

"This is a last-minute business trip. I'm staying at the new resort Liam's family built at Pleasure Cove." He tried his best to focus on his mother's face, and not the chaos surrounding them. "He wants me to work on a project for the resort. I haven't accepted the job yet, but I'm considering it."

"Really?" His mother pulled him into the room and toward the sofa. Shifting a pile of magazines from the couch to the floor, she made a place for him. She sat, then patted the space beside her. "All these years, you wouldn't take a job from the Westbrooks. Got your daddy's pride." Through years of practice she'd managed to make the last statement without malice. In fact, there was almost a hint of a smile.

Wes wished he could manage even a semblance of a smile at the mention of his father. The man that had up and left them so many years ago.

All because of him.

He cleared his throat. "I wouldn't be an employee. I'd be working with them as a contractor. And nothing is set in stone. We had the preliminary meeting earlier today."

"If it would keep you here, I'm all for it." She patted his hand and smiled. "But you seem worried. Why?"

Wes drummed the pads of his fingers against his knee. Whatever was going on with his mother, her innate sense of when he was perturbed was still intact. "It would mean working with a girl I met more than a year ago. Things didn't quite work out between us."

"Humph." She nodded, knowingly. "If you'd settle down and give me some grandchildren, you wouldn't have to worry about encountering ex-lovers at business meetings."

Wes sighed. "She isn't an ex-lover. We spent one night dancing and hanging out at a club in London. There was nothing to it really."

His mother laughed. "I'm guessing the young lady doesn't agree."

"Yeah, well it's nothing we can't work through."

"If you really believed that, you wouldn't be considering passing up on this job. And if you're considering taking money from the Westbrooks, it must be a game-changing opportunity." Her eyes twinkled. Sometimes he wondered if she didn't know him better than he knew himself.

Liam and Nigel Westbrook had been trying to get him to come on board at Westbrook International Luxury Resorts since his days in university. But he'd been a scholarship kid at the private academy he'd attended with Liam and at college after that. He didn't want a position just because Liam was his best friend. He wanted to earn his way in the world on his terms. Which was why his master's degree in business was collecting dust on the shelf in his flat back in London. During college, he'd discovered his gift for organizing events. Better still, he'd learned he could make a hell of a lot of money doing something he actually enjoyed. So he'd abandoned his plans to scale the corporate ladder at some conglomerate and struck out on his own.

As proud as Wes was of how the business had grown in London, he wanted to expand his business to the US. Another way to prove to his father that he was a success. The kind of person he should never have walked away from.

It was the only reason he'd considered Liam's offer.

Wes smiled. "Think you know everything, don't you?"

"Not everything. Just you." She squeezed his hand. "Why don't I fix us some lunch. You must be hungry."

"Don't go to any trouble on my account. In fact, why don't I take you out to eat? How about we go and grab an early dinner at the restaurant on the waterfront you're always telling me about?"

A slow smile spread across her face. "You sure? I could just as easily cook us up something. Won't take but a minute."

"I'm positive." He stood. "You go on and get ready. When we come back, I'll help with anything you need around the house."

The fair skin on his mother's cheeks pinked slightly. "I know things have gotten a little out of hand around here. Like I said, if I'd known you were coming—"

"It's okay, Mom." The last thing he'd wanted was to embarrass his mother, but there was something going on. Something she hadn't mentioned during their frequent calls. He needed to get to the bottom of it. "I haven't been home in a few years. I just want to help any way I can while I'm here."

Her smile slid back into place. "Okay, baby. Give me a few minutes to get myself together." As she stood, she seemed to lose her balance. He reached for her, but she'd steadied herself on the edge of the couch. "I'm fine." Her tone was defensive. She cleared her throat, then softened her expression. "Just the trappings of old age, I guess. I'll be back in a few. Excuse me."

He watched his mother cross the room and ascend the stairs. Her gait was unsure, and she gripped the banister as if her very life depended on it. The last time he'd visited she was practically taking the steps two at a time. Like always.

A sinking feeling settled in his gut and crept up his

spine. Wes walked back into the dining room and surveyed the books and magazines cluttering his mother's table. They were mostly health and nutrition magazines with little sticky notes protruding from them. He picked one up and turned to the marked page. A tightness gripped his chest, making it difficult for him to breathe. He put down the magazine and picked up another and another. Each sticky note marked an article about Parkinson's disease.

He shifted his gaze to the pile of books. The title on the top of the pile sent a chill down his spine. *Parkinson's Disease: A Complete Guide for Patients and Families.* The orange cover of the second book offered *300 Tips for Making Life with Parkinson's Disease Easier.*

A wave of panic rose in his chest. He steadied himself on a chair then flopped down in it. Lena Adams was one of the strongest women he'd ever known, rivaled only by his grandmother. She was wrong about Wes having his father's pride. Every ounce of strength and willfulness he possessed, he'd learned from her. She'd always seemed…invincible, so independent. Thinking of his mother slowly losing herself to this disease terrified him.

Wes heard his mother descending the creaky stairs. He should put everything back so she wouldn't know he'd been rummaging through her things, but he wouldn't. Instead, he turned to face her, brandishing the orange-covered book. "Why didn't you tell me?"

The smile on her face instantly disappeared, replaced by a look of guilt and apology. She didn't bother to chastise him for going through her books. "I—I was going to tell you the next time you brought me out for a visit."

"How long ago were you diagnosed?" He tried to keep his voice even, despite the fact he was so angry he could practically crawl out of his own skin.

Lena lowered her gaze before returning it to his. "Formally? About six months ago. I began to suspect a few months before then."

So she'd known on her last visit to London, just a few months ago. He rubbed his temple. Why hadn't he noticed?

"We need to talk about this."

Lena grabbed her purse off the chair. "No reason we can't talk and eat." Her cheeky smile almost made him laugh.

Wes looped his arm through hers and led her to the door.

"This is why I didn't tell you. You've known all of five minutes, and already you're treating me like an invalid."

"I'm not treating you like an invalid. I just want to make sure you're okay."

"I am." Her genuine smile and eyes shiny with tears warmed his chest. "Especially now that you're here."

On the ride into town, his mother chatted away, catching him up on what his aunts and cousins were up to. Her familiar laugh gave him a sense of solace. But he couldn't help noticing the slight trembling in her left hand as it rested on her knee. Or the limited gestures she used as she spoke. Both were unlike her, giving him more cause for concern.

Wes had been ready to call his friend and tell him he was passing on the project, but this changed everything. His mother needed him, whether she was willing to admit it or not. Establishing his business in the US, so close to his mother, was no longer a matter of ambition or pride.

It was a matter of family.

His mother had made so many sacrifices for him and his brother, a reality that plagued him with guilt. He'd never be able to repay her sacrifices in-kind. Didn't mean he couldn't try.

Not even if it meant checking his ego at the door and working with Bree Evans to put on the best event the Carolina coast had ever seen.

Chapter 3

Bree arrived fifteen minutes early for the meeting. Because she was always early. Also, because she hoped to get a quick word in with Wes. If they were going to work together over the next six months, she needed to keep things civil. Nothing had happened between them. Other than an amazing night together and a kiss that was so hot and sweet that it melted her insides and made her heart skip a beat.

Other than that, nothing at all.

Bex was right. She needed to let go of her resentment toward Wes. Count her lucky stars they hadn't slept together. Then things would've been unbearably awkward.

She would apologize and clear the air. Let bygones be bygones and all of those other ridiculous clichés. Not for him, but for her. Her participation in this event would expand their brand. Help her and Bex maximize the value of what remained of their careers on the volleyball circuit.

Bree entered the room. No one was there, except Lisa, who stood at the end of the table sorting documents. "Good morning, Bree. Can I get you a cup of coffee?"

"Good morning." She smiled brightly as she surveyed the chairs. Where would Wes sit? Probably next to Liam, who'd likely sit at the head of the table. She walked around the other side of the table and hung her bag on the second seat from Liam's probable chair. Lisa eyed at her expectantly. "Oh, the coffee. I'm fine. Thank you."

The corner of Lisa's mouth quirked in a knowing smile. "All right. Everyone should be here in a minute."

Bree's cheeks warmed. The other woman hadn't done a very good job of hiding her amusement over her careful deliberation about where to sit.

Note to self: take it down a notch. Your crazy is showing.

"Can I help with anything?"

"I'm about finished here." Lisa slid a few stapled sheets into a blue folder, then shut it. "There. All done."

Rather than taking a seat, Bree wandered over to the window and gazed out onto the water. She loved her life on the West Coast, but the Carolina coast was certainly beautiful, too. As soon as the water warmed up a bit, she would get out on a kayak and explore the Cape Fear River on the other side of the island. Right now, the water was still too chilly, despite the mild temperature outside.

Finally, Bree heard voices approaching. She waited until they were in the room to turn around, flashing her biggest smile. "Good morning."

"Good morning, Bree." Liam shook her hand in both of his, a gesture that was warm and welcoming. "Sorry I couldn't make yesterday's preliminary meeting. I had a family emergency, but I'm here now, and I'm thrilled you've decided to come on board with the project. It's going to be an amazing event. Good for the Pleasure Cove community and the sport of volleyball."

"I know. I'm thrilled. Thank you for inviting me to be part of it."

Miranda greeted Bree, then took the seat next to Liam, closest to the door. The seat she would've expected Wes to take. When Lisa slipped into the seat between her and Liam, that left only the seat across from her vacant. Which meant she'd spend the entire meeting pretending not to stare at him.

"Looks like we're all here," Miranda said. "Let's get started."

"What about... I mean, isn't Wes joining us?" The words spilled out of her mouth before she could stop them. She didn't dare look over at the amused half grin that was probably perched on Lisa's mouth.

Liam's eyes twinkled and his mouth pressed into a slow, subdued smile. "Wes had a family emergency of his own. He won't make today's meeting, but he should be here when we meet on Friday."

"Oh." Bree tried to filter the disappointment from her voice. She adjusted in her chair. *Way to look nonchalant.*

There was a brief moment of awkward silence that made Bree want to crawl into a ball and hide in a corner, until finally, Miranda started the meeting. She directed everyone to the agenda placed inside the front pocket of the folders in front of them.

They reviewed various possible formats for the event, based on ideas generated in the previous meeting. Miranda reviewed reports on current beach-volleyball tournaments in California and Miami Beach. Bree shared her insight on what worked at those tournaments and what could be improved, based on her participation in them in the past. Liam stressed that the event needed to entice notable celebrities who would draw people to the resort.

Lisa reminded everyone of the need to draw visitors who were not diehard fans, including locals. That was Wesley's expertise. Together they made a solid plan that they were all excited about.

After the meeting, Miranda leaned in toward Liam, her voice low. "Has Wes committed to the project?"

"Not yet. But I expect he will soon." Liam's polite smile indicated that his vague response was the extent of their discussion on the matter.

Bree had reacted badly to seeing Wes. She realized that now. Was he waffling on the project because of her?

Wes didn't seem like the kind of guy to let a little contention get in the way of something he really wanted. Still, if she was the reason he hadn't committed, it was more important than ever that she apologize to him. Before he walked away from the project.

Bree said her goodbyes and headed down the hallway.

Liam caught up with her. "Bree, can I give you a

ride to your guest house? I'm headed out for a lunch meeting."

She wanted to politely reject his offer. Spend the short walk back to her place lost in her own thoughts. Her feet, already tired of the four-inch patent-leather heels she was wearing, had other ideas. "Sure."

As they walked toward the front door, Liam stopped and turned to her. "I'm meeting with a few influential folks in town to quell their concerns about the com-mercialization of the island. It would be great if you came along. You'd be doing me a huge favor, if you don't have other plans."

She wanted to say no. She really did. But his plead-ing dark eyes and brilliant smile won her over. Be-sides, she'd taken the time to make up her face and wear a sexy outfit. She should get some mileage out of all that effort before heading back to the guest house and slipping into her comfy yoga pants and T-shirt.

"I'd love to meet some of the townspeople. Maybe even get them on board with the project early on. We're going to need a lot of volunteers."

Liam shook a finger, smiling. "I love the way you think. I owe you one."

"Two, actually." Bree held up two fingers. "The other is for not telling me Wes would be working on the project, too."

Liam pressed his mouth into a straight line, an eye-brow raised.

Busted.

"Perhaps I should've mentioned that. But I can't say I'm sorry I didn't. It would've been a shame if either of you begged off because of it. I think you two will make an excellent team." His smile widened.

She sighed. No apology, but at least he'd given an honest response. That, she could appreciate.

"You're right. I would've said no. That would've been a mistake."

Liam grinned. "You're both here. That's what matters."

Bree wasn't so sure. After all, she'd committed to the project; Wes hadn't. Maybe he'd decided that working with her wasn't worth it. She forced a smile and tried not to let the hurt that arose from that thought crack her smiling veneer.

Wes parked the Challenger in front of the guest house, stepped out of the car and stretched his long frame. He'd spent the last two nights in one of his mother's spare rooms. They had a delicious meal on the waterfront. By the time they ordered dessert she finally leveled with him about her Parkinson's diagnosis. She brought him up to speed on her doctor's prognosis and invited him to accompany her to her next doctor's appointment, which had been today.

He'd spent the last two days getting his mother's house back to the standards she'd always kept. He'd sifted through stacks of papers and mail, sorting and filing what was important, dumping what wasn't. He'd vacuumed carpets, scrubbed floors and cleaned the bathrooms and kitchen. Every muscle in his body ached. It reminded him of those brutal days on the rugby field at university. The days when he'd been sure he must be some guilt-ridden masochist to love the damn sport so much.

His mother's doctor appointment was two hours before his meeting with Liam and Bree. He'd hoped to get back in time to catch part of the meeting, but the doctor's office had used the term *appointment* loosely. By the time they got in to see the doctor, got blood tests, a CAT scan and filled her prescription, they were both exhausted. And there was no way he could make the meeting.

Bree had probably been thrilled by his absence.

Liam pulled behind his car, his face etched with concern. "You made it back. Everything all right?"

"Things have been better." Wes forced a weak smile and rubbed his hand over his head. That's when he noticed Bree sitting in the passenger seat of Liam's car. Their eyes met briefly. She forced a quick smile and nodded, then turned away.

"You look like hell. Want to talk about it?" Liam asked, before he could acknowledge the olive branch Bree had extended.

Liam was his best friend. They kept few secrets from each other. But for now, he preferred to keep the news of his mother's illness to himself. As if not talking about it made it less real. A bad dream from which he'd awaken. Besides, he didn't want to discuss it in front of Bree.

"Maybe later."

"Over golf tomorrow? Ten o'clock?"

Wes shook his head and laughed. There were few things in life Liam enjoyed as much as beating his ass in a round of golf. "Yeah, sure."

"Great. I'll pick you up then," Liam said before turning to Bree and thanking her for lunch.

He should've headed inside. After two nights in that too-little bed, he was desperate to sleep in a bed that could accommodate someone taller than a leprechaun.

Instead, he remained rooted to his spot, his feet refusing to budge, as he watched Bree exit the car. When Liam waved and pulled away, Wes didn't respond. He was focused on Bree. She looked stunning, and she seemed fully aware of it.

She strutted toward him in mile-high patent-leather heels that gleamed in the sunlight and made her legs look even longer than he remembered. The white wrap blouse hugged her full breasts, revealing a hint of cleavage. The black pencil skirt grazed the top of her knee. Each step she made offered a generous glimpse of her thigh through a slit positioned over the center of her right leg. She came to a stop in front of him. The same exotic scent she'd worn the night they met at The Alley wafted around her. Fruity and floral. He hadn't been able to get enough of that scent as he held her that night.

"Hello, Brianna." His voice came out softer than he'd intended. Wes cleared his throat and elevated the bass in his voice. "How'd the meeting go?"

"Very well. Sorry you weren't able to make it. Looks like you've been busy the past couple of days." She assessed his clothing. Same jacket and pants he'd worn during their initial meeting. Only more wrinkled.

He could only imagine what she was thinking. No point in trying to dissuade her. Besides, he didn't owe her an explanation. Wes ran a hand over his head. "Yeah, I have. It'll be good to sleep in my own bed tonight."

Her cheeks turned crimson. She bit the corner of her lip. The deep red lip color highlighted how kissable her lips were. A fact to which he could attest. "Can we talk?"

"Sure." He reached into the backseat of the car and pulled out two grocery bags. "But I have to get these groceries in the fridge. Mind stepping inside while I put them away?"

Her hair wasn't pulled back into the severe bun she'd worn earlier in the week. Loose curls cascaded over her right shoulder. She shook her head, and the curls bounced. He balled his fingers into a fist at his side at the thought of fisting a handful of her luxurious hair and taking her from behind. He swallowed, his mouth dry.

"You cook?"

He laughed. "A guy's gotta eat, right?"

"Our meals are being comped." He could hear the click of her heels against the concrete as she followed him up the path to his door.

"I know, but I felt like throwing a steak on the grill."

"In February?"

"When a February day is as beautiful as this one, why not?"

Bree followed him into the kitchen and stood beside the counter making idle chitchat as he put away the groceries. Apologizing was the right thing to do. She believed that. So why was it so difficult to say the words? The words of apology had been lodged in her throat since she noticed he was wearing the same clothes from earlier in the week. He smelled like soap. The utilitarian kind you bought in bulk. A familiar scent. It was all her family could afford when she was growing up. So he'd showered, but he'd been too preoccupied to return here for a change of clothing.

The thought of him spending the past two nights in someone else's bed caused a tightness in her chest that made it hard to breathe deeply. Which was silly. Why should it matter what Wesley Adams did in his spare time and with whom? Her only concern was his actions relating to the event. As long as he nailed this event, he could bang the entire eastern seaboard for all she cared.

The sound of Wes shutting the refrigerator door broke in to her thoughts. He gestured for her to take a seat in the living room. She sank into the cushion of the blue checkered sofa and crossed her legs.

She followed his gaze, which traveled the length of her long legs. His tongue darted out to quickly wet his lips before he dragged his gaze back to hers. "You wanted to talk?"

Her pulse quickened and she smiled inwardly. He still found her attractive. A small vindication.

Bree clasped her hands in her lap, looking down at them for a moment before raising her eyes to his. "I wanted to apologize for how I came off the other day. It was childish and petty. This project is important to both of us. If we're going to work together, I don't want things to be weird between us. So I wanted to clear the air by saying I'm sorry."

Wes seemed pleasantly surprised by her apology. He scooted forward on the couch and gave her a sheepish smile. "I accept your apology, but only if you'll accept mine. I wanted to call, I just…" He sighed, then scooted back on the couch again. His tone turned more serious. "Didn't seem like it was the right time for me."

"Oh." She hadn't meant to say it out aloud. Especially not in that sad, wounded-puppy whimper that changed his expression from contrition to pity. When he felt remorse, she had the upper hand. Now that he seemed to pity her, the power had shifted back to him. Bree shot to her feet. "No apology necessary, but thanks. I'll let myself out."

"What prompted the change of heart?"

Her hand was nearly on the doorknob, but his question grabbed her by the shoulders and yanked her back into the room. She turned back to him and shrugged. "For the sake of the project."

He took a few steps toward her. "Why were you so upset about that night?"

"Why does it matter?"

"Curious, I guess." He shoved his hands in his pockets, drawing her attention to the strain the gesture placed on the placard covering his zipper.

"I overreacted. I get cranky when I'm jet-lagged." The space between them was closing too rapidly. She took a few steps backward toward the door.

His self-assured smile suggested that her answer had told him everything he needed to know.

Her cheeks flamed and she swiveled on her heels, but before she could escape, he'd gently caught her by the hand. A familiar heat traveled from his large hand into hers, up her arm and into her chest. She raised her eyes to his.

"Look, I bought more than enough food to share. I'm going to marinate the steaks then get a few hours of sleep. But I should have the steaks on the grill at say—" Wes flipped his wrist and glanced at his watch "—seven thirty. Why don't you join me for dinner? You can assess my cooking abilities for yourself."

His wide grin and close proximity were doing

things to her she wasn't proud of. Wesley Adams wasn't a man she should be flirting with. Nor were they friends. He was a means to an end.

Bree glanced down at his hand on her arm and he dropped it to his side and took a step backward. "Thank you for the offer, but I'm pretty tired, too. I should probably just order in and get some rest."

"The invitation is open, if you change your mind."

Bree had turned and run out of there like her hair was on fire. If it hadn't wounded his pride, he would've found it funny.

Wes closed the door behind her and returned to the kitchen. He seasoned the steaks and put them into the fridge.

You invited her to dinner, genius? Really?

They were forced to work together over the course of the next six months. Like Bree said, they needed to play nice. He appreciated that she'd come to that conclusion. That she had no plans to make the next six months a living hell for both of them.

Being cordial was crucial to the success of the project. Getting to know each other, up close and personal, could only lead to trouble. Yet, he couldn't stop himself. His brain had taken a coffee break and the head on his shoulders was no longer in control.

He'd been dying for another excuse to touch her warm, soft skin. The memory of their night together in London blazed brightly in the back of his mind, like an image from an old-fashioned projector. His skin tingled with the sensation of her body pressed to his on the dance floor. Of his mouth on her lips, her neck, her bare shoulder. The unfinished business between them.

It was good Bree had turned down his invitation. Better for the both of them.

Chapter 4

For the past three hours, Bree had tried to take a nap. Instead, she tossed and turned. Thinking of him. And of that damn kiss. The one that had haunted her for more than a year.

Get your head together. It's not like you've never been kissed.

True. But she'd never been so thoroughly kissed. Kissed in a way that made every nerve in her body raw and frayed. Deeply relaxed, yet ready to spring into action. A kiss that made her want him in the worst way. Body and soul.

In that instant, she'd set aside her plan to make Wesley Adams hers for the night. She'd wanted something deeper with the guy who'd been sweet, funny and incredibly sexy. To be kissed like that for more than just one night. So she'd politely refused his invitation to go back to his place.

She'd regretted it ever since.

Given the chance again, she would've accepted his invitation. If only to ease the tension and stress that had her body strung tighter than a new volleyball net.

Bree slipped on yoga pants, a T-shirt and a hooded sweater, then went downstairs to order from one of the resort restaurants. She grabbed a bottle of water from the fridge and took a sip. A mouthwatering scent had infiltrated the kitchen.

Grilled meat.

Her belly churned. She could almost taste the steak. The one with her name on it.

Bree stepped through the double doors and onto the back deck, following the scent.

"Hey." Wes grinned. He stood over the grill on his deck in a black sleeveless shirt that showcased the gun show he called biceps. His right arm was covered with a tribal tattoo. A pair of lived-in jeans highlighted his assets.

It was colder outside than she thought. Her nipples beaded, pressing against the fabric of her bra. Bree offered a half-hearted wave, then pulled her sweater tight against her body. "Hey."

"You eat yet?" His grin widened when she shook her head. "Got your steak on the grill. C'mon over."

No. No. Tell him no.

Her brain was clear on what to do. Her belly objected, rumbling in response to the delectable aroma. "I'm ordering pizza tonight."

"Or you could have a home-cooked meal with me." His voice indicated that his option was clearly the better choice. Her roiling stomach agreed. "Besides, you're on the road a lot. Home-cooked meals must be a rarity."

"You're assuming I don't cook."

Wes raised an eyebrow, his dark eyes lit with amusement. "Do you?"

She didn't, but that wasn't the point. "It's getting late."

"You're a California girl. It's still afternoon there. Besides, it's just a meal. You can leave as soon as we're done. If that's what you'd like." He'd paused before adding that last bit.

Her jet-lagged brain struggled to manufacture another excuse. Nothing came to her. "Okay. I'll be over in a sec." She headed toward the door.

"Or you can hop the banister now." He closed the lid on the grill and held out a hand to her.

Bree chewed her lower lip as she surveyed the banister between their decks. There were wooden benches on either side of the railing. The banister was only a few feet high. She could easily jump it. Still…

She blew out a breath and stepped up onto the bench. Placing her hand in his, she stepped up onto the railing, then down onto the bench on his side. Before she could jump down, Wes planted his hands on her waist and lowered her to the floor. Taken by surprise, she gasped, drawing in his scent—clean man with a hint of juniper and sandalwood.

Bree fought the desire to lean in, her nose pressed to his freshly scrubbed skin, and inhale deeply. She tried not to muse about how delicious it felt to be back in his arms. So close that heat radiated from his brown skin. She stepped beyond his grasp, shaking her head to clear it of thoughts that would only lead to trouble. "So what's for dinner?"

Wes grinned. "Rib eyes, grilled corn, baked potatoes and grilled onions and peppers. Sound good?"

"Sounds perfect. You went all out tonight."

"Just a little something I threw together." He smiled. "Can I get you a beer or a glass of wine?"

"Red or white?"

"Pink." A wide smile spread across his face. "Sampled a great wine at the grocery store today that'll complement the steak nicely. It's chilling in the fridge now."

"I'll take the wine with dinner." If she was going to be alone with Wesley Adams for the next hour, she'd better do it mostly sober. "Can I help with anything?"

The buzzer sounded in the kitchen. "Potatoes are done. Can you take them out of the oven and plate them? Oven mitts and plates are on the counter."

She slipped inside the kitchen and did as he asked, glad to put space between them.

Bree's eyes twinkled with an excitement she seemed eager to hide as she surveyed her carefully loaded plate. She picked up her utensils. "Everything smells so good."

"Tastes even better. Dig in. Don't be shy." He couldn't peel his gaze from her face long enough to carve his own steak, afraid to miss her reaction.

Bree took a bite. An appreciative moan signaled her approval. The deeply erotic, guttural sound triggered an involuntary twitch below his belt. "This is probably the best steak I've ever had. Where'd you learn to cook like this?"

"My mom is an amazing cook. Taught me everything I know." He took a bite of the steak. It was tender and succulent. Seasoned to perfection. His mother would be proud.

"It's good she taught you to be self-sufficient. It's no picnic being with someone who isn't." Her brows knitted, as if a bad memory flashed through her brain.

"Something you know from experience, I gather." Wes sipped of his beer. He didn't want to delve deeper into her obvious pain. Yet a part of him was curious.

Bree took a generous gulp from her wineglass. "It was a long time ago."

He took the hint and changed the subject. "So how's Rebecca's shoulder? I read somewhere she'd be sidelined for at least four months."

"Could be a little longer. She's going stir-crazy, but her physical therapy is coming along."

"Good." He put butter and sour cream on his potato. "Dealing with an injury can be tough. Especially late in an athlete's career."

"Were you a soccer player, like Liam?" She dug in to her potato, already smothered in butter and sour cream.

"No, rugby was my sport."

"Amateur or professional?"

"I played at university, then on a lower tier regional league. Definitely wasn't in it for the money." He took another swig of his beer.

"Is rugby as rough as they say?"

"Worse. Got half a dozen injuries to prove it."

"Were you hurt badly?"

Wes winced inwardly at the memory of his last

injury, but shrugged nonchalantly. "Sprains and broken bones. Typical injuries in a high-contact sport."

"Is that why you quit?" She took another sip of her wine, her expressive brown eyes trained on him.

"Never really had a passion for the game. It was something to do in university and I was good at it. Mostly, it was a great way to blow off steam."

"Let me guess, you were the misunderstood rebel type." She speared a piece of steak and pointed her fork at him, then put the morsel in her mouth. His eyes followed the motion. He envied that morsel of beef as she savored it, her full lips pursed as she chewed.

"What gave it away?" He chuckled as she eyed the tattoo sleeve on his right arm, part of a large tribal tattoo that also encompassed the right side of his chest and back. "I didn't consider myself a rebel. Too cliché. On the surface, I was a pretty affable guy. Had a lot of anger pent up inside. Rugby seemed like the best way to release it."

Wes cut into his steak and took another bite, chastising himself. He'd invited Bree to dinner to repair the damage he'd caused and build a working relationship. Not to tell her his entire life story.

He seldom discussed his past with the women he dated. And never with the women with whom he did business. He preferred to stick to the casual overview. Fish-out-of-water Southern boy raised in London was usually enough.

So why had he cracked open the door to his past to Bree?

Because there was something about her that put him at ease. Made him feel like he could let down his guard. It was the thing he remembered most about that night. He was attracted to her, of course. She was Bree Evans. Tall. Gorgeous. Miles of smooth, glistening skin the shade of brown sugar. Provocative, yet sweet. She was laid-back and genuine with a smile that could convince an Eskimo to buy a truckload of ice. No wonder sponsors fell all over themselves to get her to endorse their products. Lip gloss, facial cleanser, breakfast cereal and workout contraptions.

Keep your head in the game, buddy. This isn't a date. You're only trying to create some goodwill.

She broke in to his thoughts with a tentative question. "What was it you were so angry about?"

"Life, I guess. The guys I attended boarding school with had the perfect life handed to them on a silver platter. I didn't." He shrugged. "It bugged me."

"Me, too." She was quiet, contemplative. "I was the scholarship kid at an elite private school." She winced, as if the memory caused her physical pain. "Took three buses to get there every morning, but I got an incredible education and a full ride to college because of it. Most importantly, that's where I fell in love with volleyball. That school changed my life, and I'm grateful for it."

"But…" There was something she wasn't saying. The unspoken words were so heavy and dense, they practically hung in the air between them. He should've ignored them, but the word tripped out of his mouth before he could stop it.

"It was hard being thrust into a completely different world. Especially for a gangly girl who wasn't quite sure where she fit in. Who wanted to be liked."

"How could anyone not like Bree Evans, the quintessential girl next door?" He smiled.

Bree glowered at him, then dug in to her potato. "You'd be surprised," she muttered.

Dammit. He walked right into that one. He wanted to make her forget what an ass he'd been. Now they'd come full circle right back to that night. His gut churned from the hurt in her brown eyes, when she raised them to his again.

"Look, about that night—"

Bree waved his words off as she shook her head. "It wasn't the right time for you. I know. I'd rather not talk about it."

Fine. It wasn't like the conversation was his idea of a good time, either. If she didn't want to talk about it, he sure as hell didn't.

They ate in silence for a few minutes. Then Bree engaged him in small talk about the surprisingly mild weather and her lunch with Liam and few of the locals. He nodded politely and responded appropriately. But he couldn't ignore the pain in her eyes, knowing he'd caused it.

He was his own worst enemy. Always had been.

"The time wasn't right because, for me, it never is. Not for anything serious. I'm focused on expanding my business, so I don't get seriously involved with anyone. Ever."

He studied her face, gauging her reaction and whether he should go further. Her lips were pressed into a straight line, her expression devoid of emotion.

Wes pressed his fingertips to his forehead. "When the night began, it seemed we were on the same page, but then… I don't know. It felt like you wanted more. That's not something I can give you. That's why I didn't call. Not because I don't like you. Because I like you too much to start something I can't finish."

Bree drained what was left of her second glass of wine. "Thank you for being so honest and for being so very considerate of my feelings. But I'm a big girl. I can take care of myself." She stood. "Thank you for dinner, but it's getting late. I'd better get back."

"Brianna, don't go. We were having a lovely dinner. I didn't mean to spoil the mood, but I don't want you to feel as if I rejected you. That wasn't it at all."

"I think I'm still a bit jet-lagged." Bree was a terrible liar, but he applauded her effort to remain civil. She took her dishes to the kitchen.

"I'll get it." Wes trailed her to the kitchen and stacked his plate on hers.

"Dinner was delicious. The least I can do is help with the dishes." Bree scraped his plate, then hers, and loaded the dishes into the dishwasher.

He leaned against the refrigerator, arms folded over his chest, as she put away the dirty dishes. She seemed to be processing his words as she rinsed the pots and pans.

Wes held his tongue. After all, how many times could a guy say he was sorry before the words became hollow and meaningless? More importantly, he kept his hands to himself, balled in tight fists beneath his arms.

He ignored the persistent desire to touch her. To taste her mouth and softly caress the skin at the nape of her neck, exposed by her high ponytail. To finish what they'd started that night in London.

He shifted his weight, camouflaging his body's reaction to the tactile memory and the current vision of

Bree bent over the dishwasher—her pert, round ass highlighted by a pair of snug, navy yoga pants.

Maybe they should call it a night, before he did something they'd both regret.

"I've got this. Really." He stepped toward her as she turned suddenly, nearly colliding with him. She planted her hands on his chest to brace herself from the impact. He grabbed her arms to steady her. When their eyes met, her cheeks turned crimson. She dropped her hands and stepped backward.

"Then I'll go." She headed toward the patio door.

"Wait, I'll help you over the—" Before he could get through the doors she'd planted her hands on the railing and vaulted over to the other side.

She was practically a blur as she hurried inside, tossing a final "thanks and good night" over her shoulder.

He ran a hand over his head and sighed.

Way to go, Wes.

Bree retreated to her bed. Her heart rate and breathing were still elevated from her vault over the banister and sprint up the stairs. Knees drawn to her chest, she rested her chin on them and hugged her legs.

The grown-ass woman equivalent of hiding in a corner, hugging her teddy bear.

So much for playing it cool.

She'd accepted his dinner invitation, determined to prove the past was behind them. They'd be able to forge a business relationship that was profitable for everyone involved. She needed to prove it to herself, as much as she needed to prove it to him.

Bex was counting on her to remain calm and stick

with the plan. She promised her friend she would. After all, her future was riding on this event being a success, too.

Bree groaned as she recounted the evening's events. Her plan went off the rails long before they sat down to eat. It was the moment he'd taken her hand in his, then grabbed hold of her waist. Instantly, she'd been transported to that night in London. Her attraction to him was as palpable now as it was then.

Still, she managed to pull it together and get through an hour of dinner conversation. Civilly. Without staring at his strong biceps or focusing on the rise and fall of his well-defined pecs as he laughed.

Okay, that last part had been a monumental failure. He caught her checking him out more than once.

No wonder he felt compelled to outline exactly where things stood between them. He wasn't interested in starting a relationship. A statement that was in direct opposition to the starry-eyed schoolgirl fantasy she couldn't seem to let go of.

His words made her want to crawl under a chair and hide.

He'd seen straight through her ruse, much as he had the night they first met. She'd walked into that club determined to be witty, flirtatious and cosmopolitan. All the things she wasn't. She'd been able to maintain the illusion most of the night. Until she met Wes. He was charming and funny, and he'd made her so comfortable she'd dropped the pretense and slipped back into her own skin, like a comfy pair of pj's. The facade quickly faded away, as did her illusions of being satisfied with something temporary and meaningless. She'd wanted more.

That night, for the first time in a long time, she'd been hopeful she could have it.

She'd been wrong.

Maybe she was just as wrong to think she could work with Wes and not be affected by his smile. His charm. His incredible body.

Bree shut her eyes and tried not to think of it. Or the way his hard muscles felt beneath her fingertips, both times she ended up in his arms tonight.

Stretching her legs, she reached for the remote and turned on the television.

Focus on the plan, not the man. She silently repeated the words her high-school volleyball coach would recite to her when she got too caught up with the opponent on the other side of the net.

Don't be fooled by his good looks and charm. Wesley Adams is the enemy.

A frenemy, at the very least. She'd dealt with plenty of those in her career. Had even partnered up with a couple.

Bree closed her eyes and visualized herself facing off against Wes on the volleyball court. As long as she held onto that image, she'd be good. In control of her thoughts and emotions. Her body's response.

Everything will be fine. She headed back down to the kitchen, repeating the words to herself.

She could do this. But first she needed a bottle of wine. No glass required.

Chapter 5

Wes slipped into the passenger seat of Liam's BMW a few minutes before ten and mumbled his greeting. Despite the comfortable mattress and room-darkening curtains, he would've gotten just as much sleep had he slept on a slab of cold concrete below a bustling railroad bridge. At five in the morning he gave up the pointless battle and went for a run on the beach. But his lack of sleep was catching up to him.

"You're all sunshine and roses this morning, I see." Liam grinned as he turned out of the parking lot and onto the main road. "Why do I feel there's a story involving Bree behind your obvious lack of sleep."

True. Though not in the way his friend was imagining. He'd lain awake last night, his words to Bree and her reaction to them replaying in his head on an endless loop. That was twice he tried to do the right thing where Brianna was concerned, only to have it blow up in his face. A vivid reminder of why he avoided serious relationships. He had a special gift for messing them up. It was a trait he'd gotten from his old man.

When he hadn't been thinking of Bree, he'd been worried about his mother. When sleep finally came, he dreamed of Bree's soft, warm, shapely curves stretching those poor yoga pants to their limit. A shiver ran down his spine now thinking of them.

Still, there was no way he'd give his friend the satisfaction of thinking he was right. Sliding his shades down the bridge of his nose, he peered at Liam. "So you admit that inviting Brianna and I both to work on this project was a harebrained attempt at matchmaking?"

"I'll admit nothing of the sort." His friend's voice was insistent, though the edges of his mouth quirked into an involuntary smirk. He cleared his throat and straightened his expression. "You and Bree are the best people for this project. If something more becomes of it—"

"It won't."

"Fine." Liam kept his eyes on the road ahead, another grin sliding across his mouth. "Though some might say the man doth protest too much."

"Save the Shakespeare bullshit. I'm serious." Wes sighed, softening his voice as he ran his hands through his hair. "Look, I know you see love and happy endings everywhere you look, now that you and Maya are about to get married. But I'm fine with things the way they are."

"I used to think that, too." His friend sported a self-satisfied grin. As if he was in possession of all of the universe's answers about love. If Wes wasn't so damn happy for the guy, he'd slap him on the back of his head, Three Stooges-style, and tell him to get a grip.

"I'm not just saying it." Wes stretched his long legs out and leaned into the headrest, his arms folded over his abdomen. "Not everyone is in search of love. Or even believes it exists." He muttered the last part under his breath and closed his eyes.

Liam chuckled. "I used to think that, too."

Wes brushed crumbs from his navy slacks and pushed the sleeves of his heather gray sweater up his forearms. Though it was mid-February, it was nearly seventy degrees. They had breakfast at the club before hitting the golf course. Despite Liam's reminder to bring his clubs, Wes left them back in London, hoping they'd skip the links. But Liam was two steps ahead of him. He'd purchased himself a new set of clubs and loaned Wes his old ones.

Now, he stood at the seventh green trying to line up his shot and cut in to the lead Liam was quickly building. Wes widened his stance, squared his shoulders, drew the nine-iron back above his shoulders and swung hard. He stood back and watched the ball's ascent.

Liam chuckled as the ball sailed, beautifully, but headed for the pond. It landed with an unceremonious plop, water shooting in the air. A handful of birds flapped their wings in protest to the intrusion. "Impatient as ever, I see. I've told you a million times, you can't rush the shot. Gotta let it come to you. It's a lesson that works in love, too, my friend."

Wes cursed under his breath at the wicked angle

the ball took, then groaned at Liam's brotherly advice. "Is that why we're here today? For Liam Westbrook's lessons in love?"

Liam laughed. "I don't plan to lecture you, if that's what you mean. But what kind of mate would I be if I didn't state the obvious?"

"That I'm being a general ass where Bree's concerned?" No point in beating around the bush.

"I'd have put it a bit more delicately." Liam held back a grin as he climbed behind the wheel of the golf cart. Neither of them were the kind of guys who relished sitting in the passenger seat. But the agreement was the winner of their last round drove the next time. It was a sucker bet. Liam was a far better player. Still, his pride wouldn't allow him to concede or stop believing he'd win next time. So here he was riding shotgun again.

"Bree's a great girl, Liam. You know I think the world of her. But I'm not interested in a relationship. A policy we once shared." He gave his friend a side eye, trying to rein in the green-eyed monster that gave him mixed emotions about his friend's engagement. He was happy for Liam. They were best friends. Had been since they were thirteen years old.

They trusted each other with their lives. Told each other the truth, whether they wanted to hear it or not. And if they couldn't tell each other the truth, they'd both learned to avoid the subject altogether.

Like he'd been trying to do now. Not that his friend was picking up on the hint.

"Come on. You act like I betrayed the bro code or something." Liam pulled alongside the tree and parked in the vicinity of where the ball had crossed over into the water hazard.

Liam was right. He was acting like an overgrown child whose best friend had become friends with the kid next door.

"I didn't mean it like that. I just meant, you once understood that philosophy. Lived by it faithfully. You were the one person I could count on to never give me grief about it being time for me to settle down." Wes shrugged. "I miss that luxury."

"Never thought of that." Liam folded his arms over the steering wheel. His expression was apologetic.

After a few moments of silence between them, he continued. "Back when I shared your philosophy on relationships, I truly believed we were the smartest guys around. But when I fell for Maya I discovered the truth about myself. I wasn't being brave all those years, I was afraid of being hurt again. Too cowardly to take the risk."

Wes climbed out of the cart with his club in hand and dropped his ball. Liam's revelation didn't come as a surprise. He remembered how devastated his friend had been when he discovered his off-and-on girlfriend, Meredith, had fallen for his brother, Hunter. Still, it was unsettling to hear Liam admit it.

Wes turned his back to Liam and concentrated on the game. He took his time and drove the ball again. This time it landed closer to the hole than his friend's had. He slid his club back in the bag and hopped inside the cart.

"Well played, mate." Liam's raised eyebrows knitted together, despite his compliment.

Wes laughed. "Look, I appreciate your concern. I

do. And you know I couldn't be happier for you. Maya and the girls are amazing. You're a lucky guy. So I get that you want to see me happy, too. But you're assuming I'm not. That my life is somehow incomplete."

Liam didn't respond. His silence said more than his words ever could.

Wes couldn't argue. He was content with his life the way it was, but he couldn't deny that there were nights when his bed felt cold and empty. Even on nights on the town, in a room brimming with people, he occasionally felt alone. But he'd been content to ignore those moments. To fill the empty space with a warm body or a night of laughter. "I'm focused on growing Adams Promotions and making the Pleasure Cove volleyball tournament a success. Don't have time for distractions. Got it?"

After a long pause, Liam nodded. "All right. Now, you were going to tell me why you looked so awful yesterday. What's going on? You sure as hell didn't look content then."

Wes lowered his eyes, his jaw clenching painfully. "It's my mom. She's sick."

Liam parked the cart and turned his body in the seat toward him. "Maya, the girls, and I had lunch with your mum a couple of months ago. She seemed fine."

"She's done her best to hide it." He swallowed the lump that formed in his throat. "She was diagnosed with Parkinson's six months ago."

"Did you know before you went to visit her?" His friend could understand the anger and frustration he felt. Liam's father hadn't told him about his battle with prostate cancer until he was already through his treatments and in remission.

Wes shook his head and shifted in his seat to alleviate the hole that burned in his gut whenever the inevitable thoughts of what was ahead for his mother came to mind. Increased difficulty with balance and movements. Not to mention the involuntary movements that were side effects of the most common medication given for Parkinson's. If the disease continued to progress at its current rate, she would require constant care in a few years. "She didn't want me to worry. Or to feel obligated to return to America. And she didn't want Drake to give up his career."

Liam squeezed his shoulder, forcing Wes to meet his gaze. His friend's knowing smile eased the suffocating pain in his chest. "Sounds like Ms. Lena. She's strong-willed and independent. And she loves you and your brother more than anything in the world."

"But not enough to tell us about her diagnosis." The reality of those words struck him hard. His mother had always been stubborn and determined. She'd made incredible sacrifices to give him and his brother the best life possible, regardless of the cost to her. Yet, now that she needed him, she wouldn't ask for his help. She didn't want to impose on his life. Had he made her feel that way? That she was a bother to him? Wes slumped in his seat, his gaze lowered again. He sure as hell wouldn't be winning any son-of-the-year awards.

Liam patted his friend on the back, then eased his foot onto the gas pedal, setting the cart in motion. "You know how protective your mother is of you two. Like you said, she didn't want you to worry. Besides, not telling you was probably also her way of retaining her dignity and independence. An illness like that forces us to face our own mortality. Even if it's only for a moment. It was hard for my dad. Must be pretty hard for your mum, too."

Mortality.

That word sent a chill down his spine that settled into his gut, twisting it. His mother had given him everything she possibly could. All he'd done was bring her grief. Her marriage ended because of him, and so did her dream career. It killed him that even now she was making sacrifices. She'd already done so much for them. They could never repay her, but he'd do whatever it took to try. Even if that meant moving back to North Carolina.

"Does Drake know?"

"We called him the same day I found out."

"I know how tough this must be for you and Drake. Anything you or your mum need…just say the word."

His friend's words dragged him out of his daze. Wes sat taller in his seat and nodded.

"You've already helped. If you hadn't invited me onto this project…" He shuddered inwardly, wondering how long his mother would've kept the diagnosis to herself. "I appreciate the opportunity and the generous housing offer while we work on the project. I'd only intended to stay for the weeks of our planned meetings, but things have changed. Despite what she thinks, my mother needs me."

"Will you move here permanently?" Liam couldn't hide the excitement in his voice, though he made a valiant effort.

A grin turned up one corner of Wesley's mouth. It was comforting that his best friend was eager to have him move closer. They'd been separated by an ocean most of the past five years. "I'm not ready to sell my flat in London, but I'm escalating my timeline to expand my business here in the US."

"Let me know how I can help."

"Actually, I do need one more favor." Wes hated asking his friend for special treatment. This was a business deal, and he always treated them as such. But regardless of whom he was working with, he had to act in his mother's best interest. As she'd always done for him. "I need to miss our next meeting. I'm returning to London to set the wheels in motion. Unless some emergency happens with my mother, I don't anticipate missing another."

"I understand. Of course. We'll get you the meeting notes and bring you up to speed. Communicate via email until you return."

Wes breathed a sigh of relief. "Thanks for understanding."

"Does that mean you're willing to overlook my meddling in your love life?" The smile returned to Liam's face, easing the tension they were both feeling.

Wes laughed and shook his head. "You know, after that first meeting, I'd planned to turn down the project. Bree was mad as hell about me leaving her hanging. I didn't think it was possible for us to work together."

Lines spanned Liam's forehead as he parked the cart. "And now?"

Wes stepped out of the cart and grabbed his putter. He shrugged. "Now I need to make this work. Seems she does, too. We've called a truce. She apologized for how she reacted after the meeting. I apologized for being an ass back then. I even invited her over for dinner last night."

Liam hopped out of the cart, grabbed his putter and

followed his friend onto the green. A huge grin spread across his face. "And after dinner?"

"I grilled steaks. We chatted. Everything was going well until…" Wes rubbed his neck and sighed.

"Until?" Liam raised an eyebrow.

"I wanted Bree to understand why things didn't work out between us. That it was because of me. Not because of anything she did or didn't do."

"Wait, you gave her the bloody it's-not-you-it's-me speech?" Liam scrubbed his hand down his face and shook his head. "Aww, bloody hell. What were you thinking?"

"She looked so hurt about what happened between us. I couldn't stand seeing that wounded look on her face. I had to do something to fix things between us."

"And did it?"

Wes blew out a breath, exasperated with himself. "She bolted out of the door like her hair was on fire and I was holding a can of gasoline."

Liam rubbed his forehead and took a deep breath. "Okay, so dinner didn't go so well. Next time…"

"There isn't going to be a next time." Wes turned to face his friend, needing him to understand how serious he was about this. "Bree and I came to an understanding. We both need this project, and we want it to be the absolute best it can be. But there isn't going to be a romance, maybe not even a friendship. Just a good, productive working relationship. We're both okay with that. I need you to be, too." Wes pointed a finger at his friend.

Liam snapped his mouth closed and lowered his gaze. He grunted, shoving one hand into his pocket.

He gripped his club and assumed his stance. "If that's what you want, fine. I won't interfere."

Liam's agreement was hardly convincing, but he would respect his wishes. He was sure of it. Liam struck the ball and they watched it roll, landing within a few feet of the seventh hole.

It was his turn.

Wes stood over the ball, lining up his shot. He inhaled deeply. *Focus, man. Get the ball in the cup. Simple as that.* He released his breath, drew back the club and smacked the ball, hitting it long.

Too long.

He bit back a curse and climbed back into the cart. If he could keep his foot out of his mouth and his golf ball on the green, maybe he would survive this project.

Chapter 6

It'd been three weeks since the disastrous dinner with Wesley. She hadn't seen him since. There had only been one meeting during the past few weeks, but Wes had skipped it. Probably because of her reaction to his confession that night.

The time wasn't right because, for me, it never is. Not for anything serious.

God, she felt like an idiot. She hadn't accepted his dinner invitation with the hopes of starting something between them. Still, those hopes had lingered in the back of her mind. Despite her desperate attempts to stamp them out.

There is nothing between us. Not now. Not ever.

She repeated the words in her head over and over as she jogged along the beach. Her pace quickened with each repetition, as if she was trying to outrun the words. Or maybe her feelings for him.

He's attractive. Charming. So what? I can think of half a dozen guys who are, too. Guys who are actually interested in me.

Bree came to a halt, as if she'd run into a solid brick wall. The phone calls from her ex that she hadn't returned, along with a text message she'd left unanswered, were vivid in her mind. She could practically hear Alex Hunt's voice, low and gravelly, uttering the words he'd typed that morning.

Been calling you. You're not at your place. Where are you? I'll only be in town for a few more days. We need to talk.

A knot tightened in her stomach. Her muscles tensed and her palms felt clammy, despite the cool breeze blowing across the water onto the beach. Bree calmed her breath and stood tall, stretching her arms toward the sky for a beat before resuming her run.

She was in control. Not Alex. It'd been more than three years since she'd ended their relationship. They were over and there was no way she was going back to him. Ever.

Still, she couldn't deny the unease she felt at his words. How did he know she wasn't at her place? And why, after three years, would he suddenly call? Had he conveniently forgotten how things had ended between them? With her threatening to get a restraining order.

Alex had taken a job in Kansas City not long afterward. She hadn't seen or heard from him since then.

Her threats of filing a complaint against him had obviously worked. So why was he contacting her now?

The truth was, she didn't care and had no desire to find out. She wasn't afraid of Alex. She'd taken defense classes. She could take care of herself if she needed to. Yet, she'd scrapped her plans to return to California and opted to stay at the resort instead. Liam had comped their housing through the wrap-up meeting following the volleyball tournament, not long after Labor Day. She hadn't intended to take him up on it. But when she heard Alex's voice mail, her blood had run cold. She'd canceled her flight home and hired a trainer to work with her in Pleasure Cove.

Bree came to a stop, hands on her hips, sweat running down the side of her face. She checked her pulse. Good, but not great. Breathing heavily, she plopped down into the sand and pulled her cell phone out of her armband and checked her email. Her sporting-goods sponsor was making the final decision on a new line of volleyball attire branded with her name. She needed to review the designs and give her input on which pieces should make the final cut.

No email from the sponsor yet. There was an email from Lisa Chastain with the subject "Changes to Program." She scanned the email, her heart beating faster.

That jerk.

Wes apparently hadn't liked her idea about making the event a family-friendly one. It wasn't part of the original plan, but it was important to her and Bex. They planned to lead volleyball camps for kids aged eight to seventeen. What better way to build a relationship with her target clients than to involve them in the Pleasure Cove tournament?

Wes clearly didn't agree. Was this his way of getting back at her?

Only one way to find out.

Bree searched the tournament contact list for Wesley's number. She inhaled a deep breath, then clicked on the number. The phone rang several times then went to voice mail.

"Hey, this is Wes. Not available right now, but leave me a message, and I'll get back to you."

The beep sounded and her heart stuck in her throat, leaving her speechless for a moment. "Wesley, this is Brianna Evans. I just saw the email about the changes you're requesting. I'd like to discuss it. Please call me back as soon as you get a moment."

Bree finished her run, determined not to think of Wes or Alex.

Five hours later, Wes hadn't answered her original message or picked up the two times she'd called since then. Maybe her behavior was coming dangerously close to that of a stalker. Bree didn't care. This was important. There was no way Liam would side with her over Wes. Miranda and Lisa were enthusiastic about her idea during the meeting, but she doubted they'd have much sway over their boss if he was backing Wes on this.

She had to go directly to the source. Make Wes understand why the family-friendly component of the tournament was critical.

Bree sat at the kitchen counter, tapping her short nails against the granite. Wes had returned to London for the past few weeks, but she'd seen him arrive the day before. He was right next door, ignoring her calls.

Bree could hear Bex's voice in her head.

Whatever it takes.

She sighed, then hopped down from the stool. Wes wasn't answering his phone. Maybe he would answer the door instead. Bree knocked. No answer. She'd smelled food grilling earlier. Maybe he was out back. Bree headed through her guest house and went outside. She looked over the barrier between their back decks. There he was, lounging on a chaise, eyes closed and earphones plugged in.

Bree called his name, but Wes didn't respond or even move an inch. She called him again. Still, he didn't hear her. Finally, she climbed over the barrier. She reached out to shake his arm, but she paused, taking him in.

God, this man is gorgeous.

The temperature was only in the low seventies, but the sun still shone brightly overhead, making it feel much warmer. He'd taken off his shirt and thrown it across the empty chaise. She studied his inked, brown skin. The tattoo on his right arm was part of a much larger tattoo that covered the entire right half of his torso and disappeared below the waistband of the swim shorts, which hung dangerously low on his hips. Just how far down did that tattoo go?

You're not here to ogle him. Get a grip.

Wes cleared his throat. A smirk curled the edges of his mouth.

Damn. Busted again.

"Hey, I was just… I mean I was…" Bree sucked in a deep breath, willing herself to stop babbling. "You didn't answer any of my calls."

"Exactly how many times did you call?" There was slight tension in his voice.

Yep. He definitely thought she was stalking him.

"A couple times," she lied, clearing her throat. "Were you screening my calls?"

"Phone's in the house. Sometimes I like to unplug." He yawned, then shielded his eyes from the sun as he looked up at her. "You should try it some time."

Bree stepped forward, her back molars grinding and her hands balled into fists at her side. "I'll pass on the life advice, thanks. It's bad enough you're taking over my event."

"*Your* event?" Wes raised an eyebrow in slight amusement as he adjusted the chair into a sitting position. "This is Liam's event. You're the celebrity name with the pretty face they hired to front the operation." A smirk lifted the corner of his mouth. "Didn't expect we'd see you beyond the first meeting."

Wes was enjoying making her crazy. If the racing of her pulse and the tightening of her nipples were any indication, he was making her crazy for him, too.

Bree tore her gaze away from the sexy smirk on his lips and forced it upward to meet his, rather than downward to steal another glance at the hard muscles glistening beneath a slight sheen of sweat.

Her nails dug into her palms as she stepped closer. Her shadow fell across him. "This isn't my first rodeo, cowboy. Contrary to what you might think, I'm *not* just a pretty face. I agreed to join this project because Liam wanted my input."

"I was only teasing. Thought it would lighten the mood." His expression was apologetic. Seemingly sincere. He snatched his shirt off the empty chaise and extended his hand toward it. "Why don't you have a seat?"

"I don't want to sit. I want to know why you've vetoed my idea without the courtesy of an email or a phone call." Bree crossed her arms over her chest, where his eyes had wandered momentarily.

Wes climbed to his feet and stretched, giving her an excellent view of the hard muscles of his chest and abdomen, beneath his smooth brown skin.

The man took good care of himself. From head to toe. No doubt about that.

He walked over to the hot tub near the far corner of the deck. After removing the cover, he folded it and placed it on the bench before slipping inside. He closed his eyes as he sank deeper into the bubbling water. The tension seemed to disappear from his shoulders.

Finally, he acknowledged her again, though he didn't open his eyes. "If you want to discuss the idea now, I suggest you grab a swimsuit. Because for the next hour or so, this is where I'll be taking my meetings."

Bree's cheeks flamed and her heart beat so loudly Wes could probably hear it. Her hands tightened into fists at her side, itching with a desire to smack that self-satisfied grin off his handsome face. "I am *not* getting into that hot tub."

"Then I guess we'll talk about this when I return in a week."

"Wesley Adams—"

He gestured that he couldn't hear her, then slipped lower in the water.

Bree gritted her teeth, climbed back over the divider and headed up to her bedroom. If he thought he could drive her off that easily, he was in for a rude awakening.

Wes shut his eyes and allowed the heated water and full-blast jet streams to melt the tension. For as long as he could remember, any stress he was feeling had gone straight to his shoulders. He could still hear his teacher, Ms. Lively, scolding him for hunching his shoulders around his ears, like they were a pair of earrings.

He'd been a sensitive kid. Always in tune with the feelings of others. Particularly his mother and grandmother. His mother had always put on a brave face and tried to hide her anxiety. But she didn't fool him. Not for a minute. Not even when he was twelve.

Over the years he'd learned to control it. To dial back his reaction to other people's feelings. He reserved that kind of investment for the people who really mattered to him.

Lena Adams was at the top of that list.

Despite the brave face she'd put on, she was scared. Afraid of what the future held when her body no longer complied. The pain that simmered beneath her brave smile nestled in his gut like a five-hundred-pound boulder. He hadn't been able to shake it.

The trip back to London hadn't helped. His event manager, Nadia, wasn't happy about his decision to make Pleasure Cove the new home base of the company. She was aware that he'd planned to expand to the US, but she'd expected him to continue living and working in London for the majority of the year. He had, too. His mother's illness changed his plans.

He wouldn't move to New Bern, where his mother lived. She'd feel he was encroaching on her independence. Instead, he'd make Pleasure Cove his home base, keeping him within an easy two-hour drive of his mother. Besides, with Pleasure Cove as his base he could easily work with Westbrook International Luxury Resorts on future projects, while slowly expanding his reach along the East Coast. It wasn't the fancy, New York office he'd planned, but he'd make it work.

"Looks like you're deep in thought. Hope you're thinking about why my family-friendly tournament is the better option."

His eyes fluttered open. Wes blinked. Twice.

Bree stepped down from the bench in a sexy, black one-piece swimsuit that caused all of the tension that had drained from his shoulders to settle below his waist. He swallowed hard as she walked toward him. The asymmetrical swimsuit had one strap, across her left shoulder. Just below her full breasts, a cut-out veered in, nearly to her navel, then dipped back out again at her waist, revealing the smooth, brown skin on the left side of her torso. Her hair was pulled up in a loose ponytail, high at the back of her head.

She was gorgeous. From the sway of her generous hips and the sly turn at the corners of her pouty lips, she damn well knew it.

The gloves were off, and Bree was prepared to play dirty. There was no way in hell he could concentrate on business while she was standing there in…*that*.

His appreciative assessment of the swim attire clinging for dear life to her undulating curves hadn't gone unnoticed. Bree tried to swallow a grin as she inched closer, then slid out of her sandals.

Wes extended his hand to her, but didn't stand. If he did, his appreciation for her choice of swimwear would become painfully obvious. "You took me up on the offer. Didn't think you would."

"Don't underestimate me. I don't give up so easily." She settled into the seat across from his.

He nodded, his gaze settling on her fiercely determined one. Bree was ready for a battle. "I know. Watched you play for years. I've seen you dig out of some tough spots. Your refusal to concede, it's what I admire most about you as a player."

"But not as a colleague seated across the boardroom table, I take it." She folded her arms beneath her breasts, inadvertently providing him with a spectacular view of her cleavage. His gaze dropped there momentarily and she immediately realized her mistake. Bree lowered her arms and narrowed her gaze at him, one eyebrow raised.

"I appreciate tenacity, even in an opponent. Regardless of the playing field. Apparently you do, too. You teamed up with one of your fiercest rivals, Bex Jacobs." Wes reached behind him and opened the cooler. "Beer?"

She stared at him for a moment, as if the question was a test, then nodded. "Yes, thank you."

Wes grabbed two beers, opened them both and handed one to her. "So you and Bex…how'd that happen?"

"We became friends during a trip to the Olympics with other partners. A couple years later, we both found ourselves in need of new partners. Teaming up was a no-brainer."

"A lot of pundits felt it was a mistake for you two to team up."

"Reporters and analysts who were afraid that without our rivalry, there would be nothing else in women's volleyball to talk about." She practically snorted. He held back a grin. "They were wrong."

"They were, and so was I. I was one of those people who thought it was a mistake. Glad I was wrong." He sipped his beer.

"But you're not wrong now?" She narrowed her gaze when he gestured that her estimation was correct. Her cheeks turned deep red and she pursed her lips. "You summarily dismissed the idea without giving it any consideration."

"I have considered your proposal. It's admirable you want to make the event welcoming to families, but that isn't what we're going for here."

"Why not? Because you say so?" She crossed her arms again, higher this time, blocking his view of her curves. It was a move he appreciated—he didn't need the distraction.

"Because we want to make as much money on this event as possible the first time out. We won't do that selling cotton candy and ice cream. Alcohol—" he held up his bottle for emphasis "—*that's* where we'll make our money. Throw in a celebrity chef making gourmet meals. Couple that with overpriced drinks with fancy names. Suddenly we're making money hand over fist our first year."

"You act like there isn't money to be made in family entertainment." The pitch of her voice climbed higher. "Ever heard of theme parks?"

"Of course." He smiled inwardly. She was on the

defensive. Not as calm and collected as she'd been when she'd strolled across the deck. "But this ain't a theme park, darlin'. The Pleasure Cove Luxury Resort is geared toward entertainment of the adult variety. I imagine having Junior underfoot would kill Dad's buzz while he's ogling the celebrity volleyball players."

She folded her arms, lifting her breasts again. Then she dropped them and sighed, not responding. He wasn't sure if she was angry with him or herself.

Despite what she seemed to think, he got no joy from raining on her parade. He'd much prefer to see that gorgeous smile of hers. The one that went straight to his chest and made his heart skip a beat.

Wes leaned in, his voice apologetic. "Look, I admire your idea. I'm just not sure there's a market for a family-friendly volleyball tournament. If there is, it's definitely not Pleasure Cove. Besides, our goal is to make this event rival some of the other popular East Coast volleyball tournaments within the next three years. Inviting small children isn't the way to do that."

Her lower lip jutted out a bit. Even her pout was sexy as hell. It made him want to cross to her side and suck on her lower lip. Hear the soft moans that would emanate from her throat when he did. The memory of how she felt in his arms and the taste of those sweet, kissable lips crawled over his skin, unsettling him.

Keep your hands and lips to yourself, man.

Wes set his beer on the hot tub, dragging his gaze back to her eyes. He hated to see her disappointed. Hated being the cause of it. But he was hired to do a job. Not to protect the volleyball princess's feelings.

So why did he feel like shit for killing her idea?

Bree set her beer bottle on the side of the hot tub. "Then we should be more aggressive with our plan. Give it a music festival vibe. Maybe bring in some up-and-coming local bands on rotating stages. That's what they did at the tournament in LA. I played in that tournament a few times. The lure of the bands boosted attendance."

"This isn't LA. We're not exactly known for our music scene."

"Okay, maybe not Pleasure Cove, but we could expand the reach to the rest of the state." She sighed in response to his unconvinced expression. "Are you saying North Carolina doesn't have the talent to pull this off?"

"Not at all. There are a wide range of talented acts here in the state. But it wouldn't have the kind of draw the LA music scene does. We can integrate local acts, maybe have them featured at some of the smaller venues, but we'll need some heavy hitters, including a highly recognizable act to anchor the center stage. I know you're a California girl, but the East Coast has a totally different vibe."

"Well, at the event in New York—"

He shook his head, ignoring the frown tugging at the corners of her mouth. "This isn't New York, either. We're in the Carolinas. Got no illusion we can beat New York or LA at their own game."

Bree folded her arms again. "Then exactly what do you suggest?"

Wes smiled, waving a hand toward the beach. "We create a competitive advantage based on what sets North Carolina apart."

"And exactly what is that?" She stared at him, one eyebrow raised. Ready for battle.

He chuckled. "The fact that you have to ask means a little research is in order."

"You're giving me homework?" The tension in her voice spiraled.

"I'm giving *us* homework." His brain immediately balked at the statement. He was supposed to be creating distance between him and Bree Evans. Not finding a way to spend more time with her. It was a battle his good sense was losing. He raised his chin. "Spend the next week exploring the state with me."

Her mouth opened and her eyes widened, but she didn't speak. She was considering it. That was more than he'd hoped for. So he pressed further.

"We'll spend a couple of days at the beach, a few in the mountains, and a day or two in Raleigh, Chapel Hill and Charlotte. You'll get a sense of what makes the state unique." She narrowed her gaze at him, so he added, "I'm a North Carolina native, but I've lived in London most of my life. The state is growing rapidly, and so much has changed. That's why I need the refresher. What do you say? Do we have a date?"

Wes regretted his word choice nearly the moment he'd uttered it.

This would be a business trip. Plain and simple. He wouldn't spend the next six months fighting her on every decision they had to make about the tournament. Which celebs to invite. The selection of celebrity chefs. Which bands to hire. Themes. The schedule.

Bree knew volleyball tournaments. She'd competed in plenty of them, competitive and exhibition. But if he could give her a better sense of the venue and what he and Liam were trying to accomplish, she might come around and stop fighting him.

Wes tilted his head, taking her in. This might be the worst idea he ever had. Bree was smart and beautiful. Yet, she was a fierce competitor. Everything about this woman made him want her.

He gripped the sides of the hot tub, determined not to move, when what he really wanted was to take her in his arms and kiss her again. Then take her to his bed.

The physical attraction was enough to battle, but what worried him most was his growing need to be in her company. He felt at ease with Brianna. Her company was a welcome antidote to the anxiety he felt over his mother's illness.

If they could get past the awkwardness of what had happened in London, maybe they could be friends.

"C'mon, it'll be fun."

She raised her gaze to his. "And we'll have separate rooms?"

"Of course. I'll be on my best behavior. I promise."

"Fine." Bree stepped out of the hot tub and dried herself off. She wrapped a towel around her body and secured it. "Email me the itinerary."

She didn't wait for his response, so he didn't offer one. He only hoped he wasn't making another huge mistake that would land both of them in hot water.

Chapter 7

"You agreed to do what?" Bex's voice blared through the speaker on Bree's cell phone, which was propped on the bathroom sink as she detangled her shoulder-length, curly hair. It was a task that took far longer than she cared to admit. "Have you lost your freaking mind? You've got a thing for this guy. Or are we still pretending that you're over him?"

"Hey, you're the one who said do whatever it takes to make this work. That's what I'm doing. Or have you forgotten the plan?" Bree responded, her heart racing. Not because she was arguing with her best friend. Because Bex was right, and they both knew it.

"I know what I said, but I also know you. The girl who wears her heart on her sleeve, and who is really attracted to this guy." Bex sighed. "I don't get this guy. First, he tells you he doesn't believe in anything serious. Next, he's inviting you to spend a week with him exploring North Carolina. What the hell? Is this some kind of sick mind game?"

"Doesn't seem like his style. Besides, now that I've had time to think about it, he's right. I need a better understanding of the locale. Maybe I've been approaching this the wrong way."

"See, that right there is what I'm talking about. He's got you doubting yourself. I thought the plan was to see him as a competitor. The enemy." Bex's Yorkshire terrier, Sheba, barked frantically in the background. Her friend was likely pacing the floor and gesturing wildly, working the poor thing up.

"And don't we always say we need to know our enemy in order to defeat him?"

"If you really mean it, it's a good plan," Bex conceded. "But it feels like you're trying to convince yourself. Are you sure this isn't just about spending some alone time with Wesley Adams?"

Bree stared at herself in the mirror for a moment before dropping her gaze to the phone. "I'm sure."

"Then good luck, but you call me the second you feel yourself falling for this guy. I'll knock some sense back into you, even if I have to fly out there." The smile was back in her friend's voice.

They both laughed. "Promise."

"Good. Anything else I should know about?"

Bree's gut churned. Was she that transparent?

She hadn't told Bex about the messages from her ex. Bree knew how her best friend would react. Without knowing some of the uglier details of the breakup three years ago, Bex had been ready to take a bat to Alex's precious car.

It was just a few voicemails and a text message. He'd get bored and give up when she didn't respond. So why get Bex upset for nothing? Besides, she didn't want to talk about Alex. She'd given him three years of her life, and he didn't deserve another moment of it.

"Everything is fine."

"You're a terrible liar, Brianna Evans," Bex said. "But whether it's Wes or something else that's bothering you, I'm here when you're ready to talk."

Bree ended the call and hoped like hell that everything would be all right.

Wes leaned against the hood of the car, his hands shoved into his pockets as he waited for Bree.

An entire week together. Alone.

What had he been thinking when he proposed this trip?

That there was no way in hell Bree would agree to his request. If he'd bet money on it, he'd have lost his flat back in London and everything in it, because Bree called his bluff. Which left him no choice but to go through with it.

Not one of my better ideas.

Nor was it part of some calculated grand plan. He'd planned this trip two weeks ago, only he'd intended to travel solo. After two decades of living abroad, he was out of touch. He needed this research trip as much as Brianna did. Besides, time on the road alone would've given him a chance to clear his head, still spinning from the reality of his mother's illness.

Then there was the dark truth that he didn't dare admit, not even to himself.

He wanted an excuse to spend time with Bree.

A small part of him hoped that the competitive spirit that made Bree Evans a world class athlete would prompt her to accept his challenge.

Wes glanced at his watch. Five minutes past their scheduled departure.

Maybe she planned to leave him waiting—her retribution for how he'd treated her in London.

Served him right. He'd been an ass, even if he'd done it for the right reasons. Then he heard her voice.

"Sorry I'm late. My mom called as I was leaving." Bree pulled a small carry-on bag behind her. Slim, dark-wash jeans hugged her luscious curves. She wore a red-and-white striped blouse with a wide band at the waist.

"Is everything okay?" He opened the trunk.

"She needed to vent. My dad retired late last year, and he's driving her crazy." A tentative smile settled on her glossed lips.

"That all you're bringing? We'll be gone a week, you know?"

"I have everything I need. When you schlep your own luggage as much as I do, you learn to pack light."

Bree eschewed his offer to take her bag. She lifted the small, black bag into the trunk. The band at her waist rose, providing Wes with a glimpse of the tattoo on her lower right side. A vibrant, purple butterfly landing on a lotus blossom rendered in a deep, rich shade of pink. He'd seen dozens of glossy photos of Bree online and in magazines. That tattoo hadn't been in a single one. He would've remembered. So it was a recent addition. Or maybe she'd always had it airbrushed out of her photos.

What does it mean?

Asking was out of the question. Might as well confess he'd been gawking at her. Not a good move at the outset of their strictly business road trip.

"You're traveling light, too." Her voice broke into his thoughts.

"I'm a simple guy." He closed the trunk and resisted the inclination to open her car door. After her insistence on handling her own luggage, he doubted she'd welcome the action. Instead, he gestured toward the car. "Shall we?"

"Sure." An uneasy smile curled the edges of her mouth. The bravado she'd shown earlier was gone, if only for a moment.

It was a feeling he knew well. They weren't on the road yet, and already the tension crept up his spine.

"Have you eaten?" When she indicated that she had, he slid behind the steering wheel and secured his seat belt. She did the same. "Good. We can hit the road right away. Got a long drive to Asheville."

"I've always wanted to visit there." Her smile deepened into one that lifted her cheeks and lit her eyes from within.

There's that smile. The one he remembered so fondly from their night together in London.

"Good, because we're spending two days there." Wes turned the ignition, then headed onto the road.

"I noticed." She waved a copy of the trip itinerary he emailed her because she'd insisted on one. It was pretty vague. Just a list of the cities he planned to visit and the dates they'd be there. "You're not a man of many details, are you?"

Wes laughed. "You'd be surprised to learn that I'm

known for my attention to detail. It's an essential skill in planning and promotions."

"So this list is purposely vague?" She held up the sheet again.

"I was going for Man of Mystery. Apparently, I've failed miserably." He smiled. "So you'll just have to take my word for it."

Bree's laughter warmed his chest. "So, Man of Mystery, what will we be doing in Asheville for two whole days?"

"Everything." He wished he could rescind the word when her shoulder stiffened and her cheeks turned crimson. "I mean, there's a lot to do there. Two days will barely scratch the surface. Got a few activities planned, but I don't want to ruin the surprise."

"Fair enough." Bree stuffed the piece of paper back into her purse, then dropped her bag on the floor. "How long until we're there?"

"It's nearly a six-hour drive."

Her eyes widened in protest. For a moment, he thought she might bolt from the moving vehicle. He held back a chuckle.

"Don't worry, we'll stop for lunch in Raleigh. Give you a chance to stretch your legs out and sample some of the best barbecue in the state."

"Raleigh's in central North Carolina. So will we be having Eastern or Western-style barbecue?"

"Someone's been doing her research."

"You said I didn't know enough about the state." She shrugged. "I decided you were right."

They were silent for a few minutes, then he asked the question that had lingered in his mind from the moment she agreed to the trip.

"So…why'd you change your mind about joining me on this trip?" Liam would accuse him of looking a gift horse in the mouth. Still, he needed to know.

"Other than the fact that you asked me?" She stared out of the passenger window.

He grinned. "Yeah, besides that."

"Partly because you didn't expect me to say yes. Partly because you were right. We can't beat the Miami or LA tourneys at their own game. We must focus on what sets Pleasure Cove apart. I need a better understanding of the location in order to do that."

"Is that why you haven't gone home between the meetings?"

She didn't reply right away, and he nearly regretted asking. What business was it of his if she hadn't returned home? Yet, when Liam mentioned it, in passing, he couldn't help wondering why she'd stayed.

"Sorry, it's none of my business."

"No, it's fine. I just wondered how you… Ahh, Liam."

Shit.

Should've kept his mouth shut. Now she'd think they were a couple of gossiping men. "We talked while I was in London. He mentioned he saw you at lunch."

She nodded thoughtfully, though he wasn't sure if she accepted his explanation or was simply acknowledging that she heard it. "I was able to conduct all of my meetings via phone or email. Since I had no pressing issues back home, I stayed put. It gave me a chance to familiarize myself with the venue and some spots around town."

"And what do you think of Pleasure Cove?" He was

glad to sway the conversation from the fact that he'd been keeping tabs on her.

"The town or the resort?"

"Both."

"The town is idyllic. Charming. There's an eclectic mix of locally owned shops and eateries along the beach and downtown. I admire the fact that they've kept the big-box stores and chains at bay. A lot of those small, quaint shops couldn't stay afloat if they had to compete with them."

"You have been getting to know the locals. And what you say is true. But their reluctance to change also left the town outdated, almost losing its relevance except with the handful of tourists who've been coming here for years, many of them since they were kids. A lot of the old guard fear the evils of commercialization, but the town and its economy needed the shot in the arm that infusion of cash brought."

"I've heard a few debates about it in town. So I understand the careful balancing act we have to do. We have to find a way to bring in the masses without pissing off the locals. That's why I thought a family-friendly event would work best. It's something everyone in town could enjoy."

It was too early in the trip to get into a heated debate about the format of the tournament again. Bree took the hint and changed direction.

"That reminds me, I think we should source goods and services for the event locally. It won't be feasible in every instance, but it may buy us some goodwill with the locals. Besides, it's just the decent thing to do."

"Great idea. My go-to vendors are all in the UK. I

need to build a database of stateside vendors anyway. I'd love to patronize local shops."

"Good to know you don't disagree with all of my ideas."

Don't take the bait, man.

An uncomfortable silence settled over the car. Wes turned on the radio and focused on the road.

Maybe their trip wasn't off to a stellar start, but he had seven days to convince Bree they were on the same side.

Chapter 8

By the time they arrived in Raleigh, Bree was restless. Their conversation had been cordial, but thankfully there hadn't been much of it during the two-hour drive up I-40W. She'd taken a series of business calls.

Wes probably thought she was being rude. If he did, she couldn't blame him. Under normal circumstances, she would've waited until she arrived to take the calls in private. However, the creative department for her biggest sponsor—a major athletic-wear line—was in a panic.

Already three weeks behind schedule getting to production, her latest sportswear line hit another snag. The team was in crisis mode.

"We're here." Wes pulled into a recently vacated parking space on the street.

"Perfect timing." Bree hit Send on the follow-up

email to the call that had lasted nearly an hour. She shoved her tablet in her bag. "I'm done with work and I'm starving."

"Me, too." Wes stepped out of the car and came around to open her door. A wide smile lifted the corners of his sensuous mouth as he extended his hand to her.

Bree slipped her hand into his. A slight shiver trailed up her arm and his scent enveloped her.

She'd been aware of his masculine scent as they rode in the car, but it was subtle. Standing toe-to-toe with him, she was enraptured by the scent. She inhaled the notes of lavender, orange and patchouli, her eyes fluttering closed for the briefest moment. Bree withdrew her hand from his and stepped away, hitching her purse on her shoulder.

Wesley's gaze dropped to the stretch of skin the movement left exposed at her waist. His eyes traced her tattoo. A butterfly alighting on a lotus blossom. Warmth filled her cheeks.

"Sorry, I didn't mean to stare. It's a beautiful tattoo. The colors are exceptionally vibrant, and it fits you."

"Thanks." She tugged down her blouse.

You are not attracted to him. You are not attracted to him. You are not...

Who was she kidding?

Of course she was attracted to Wesley Adams. He was tall, dark, handsome and incredibly fit. A fact not hidden by the gray, lightweight sweater he wore over a pale blue button-down shirt. His dark eyes, framed by neat, thick brows, seemed to stare right through her, exposing her every thought and emotion.

Bree folded her arms and nodded toward a redbrick-

and-glass building that looked like a converted warehouse. "This the place?"

A stupid question, but she needed to say something. *Anything.*

"You bet." Wes placed a hand low on her back as he steered her out of the way of a group of people who'd spilled out of the restaurant and onto the sidewalk. "Just wait until you try the chopped barbecue and fried okra."

Bree tried to ignore the heat seeping into her skin and the way her body reacted to his touch.

"Not a fan of okra. It's so…slimy. Human food should not be slimy."

The laughter that rumbled in his chest vibrated against her shoulder. "I don't disagree. In fact, the only way I'll eat it is fried." He ushered her inside.

"I'm not eating anyone's okra." Her tone was definitive.

"That'd be a shame, 'cause our okra is awful good." A gorgeous blonde with sparkling blue eyes flashed her brilliant teeth in a good-natured smile.

"I'm sure it is." Bree tucked her hair behind her ear. "It's just not my thing."

"We got a menu full of options. You'll have plenty to choose from."

They settled into their booth and Bree scanned the menu.

"We can order whenever you're ready." Wes sipped his water.

"You haven't touched your menu."

Wes grinned. "Don't need it. I know exactly what I want."

* * *

He hadn't intended to, but as Bree studied the options, her gaze buried in the menu, Wes took the opportunity to study her.

For a moment, why he'd chosen not to call her escaped him.

Right. Because he didn't want to be the asshole who broke the heart of America's volleyball sweetheart.

Being the good guy didn't always pay off.

Bree tugged her full, lower lip between her teeth as she studied the menu.

Sensory memories of that night in London flooded his brain. The flavor of Bree's lip gloss. The warm, sweet taste of her mouth. How her body—with its perfect mix of lean muscles and sexy curves—pressed against his. His pulse raced and heat crawled up his neck.

I'm a bloody masochist.

No other way to explain why he'd torture himself by inviting Bree Evans on this trip.

"I've heard about this place." Excitement lit her brown eyes. "It's supposed to be really good."

"One of the best around. I come here whenever I'm in town."

"You've been living in London. How often do you get to Raleigh?"

"Whenever I visit my mother, we make it a point to come here at least once." He drummed his fingers on the table. "Truthfully? Not often enough. I usually fly Mom out to visit me. I haven't been too keen on returning home."

"Why?" Her intent gaze penetrated him.

He opened his mouth to deliver his usual excuse,

that he had been busy, but there was something about Bree. He didn't want to bullshit her. Still, there was no need to relive his entire life story.

Wes rearranged the salt and pepper shakers. "Running from bad memories, I guess."

"Sorry." Bree lowered her gaze. "I shouldn't have pried. I didn't mean to dredge up bad memories."

"No need to apologize. You couldn't have known." He forced a smile, hoping to set her mind at ease. "You know, I haven't thought of New Bern as home in years. I spent most of my life in London and it's felt like home for the past twenty years, but…"

"But this trip home feels different?" Her wide, brown eyes were like a truth elixir.

Wes nodded. "Yeah. When I first got off that plane last month, it was the first time since I was a kid that I felt some sense of nostalgia. Maybe even a little bit of homesickness."

"So will you be coming home more often now?"

"Actually, I decided to move back to the US. I've always known that one day I wanted to establish my event-and-promo business here." Wes dropped his gaze from hers. He wouldn't lie to her, but she wasn't entitled to know everything about him or his family. "Now feels like the time to do that."

"Your mother must be happy."

"Haven't told her yet. I wanted to wait and see how things worked out with the tournament."

"You mean whether you could stand to work with me for an entire six months." She laughed when his eyes widened. "Relax, I'm not offended. I considered backing out, too."

"I'm glad you didn't." His gaze held hers. His pulse

quickened in response to the slow smile that spread across her face.

"Glad you didn't, either." Bree tucked her hair behind her ear. "I think we have the potential to be an incredible team that delivers on everything Liam is hoping for, but that means we need to function like a team. No surprises."

"Fair enough," Wes conceded, thankful the server stepped in to take their order.

Once their orders were complete, she checked her email again.

"Everything okay with your sponsor?" Wes sipped his sweet tea. "I couldn't help overhearing some of your conversation in the car."

"The usual production drama." She shrugged, putting her phone on the table. "Seems there's some sort of drama whenever we roll out a new line. I've learned to roll with it. What about you? Seems like you had some business drama of your own."

"Got a big corporate event coming up. I'll be there for the event and the days leading up to it, but I'm letting my team take the lead on this one. I've been dealing with this client for a while. He's having a bloody meltdown, as he's wont to do during these events."

"But you weren't speaking to him. You were speaking to a woman."

"How'd you…?"

"You turn up that Southern-boy charm when you're speaking to a woman." The corner of her mouth curved in the sexiest smirk he'd ever seen as she swirled her straw inside her glass. "Even if you're not attracted to her."

Wes didn't acknowledge her assessment as he

leaned back against the booth. What she'd said was true, though not something he did intentionally.

"I was talking to my event manager, Nadia. She's second-in-command. She's bright and capable, but she's nervous about taking over the reins."

"Oh." She seemed relieved by his answer. "I liked how you handled the conversation. You conveyed your confidence in her in a way that felt warm and genuine. It seemed to calm her down. I couldn't hear *what* she was saying, but I noticed the shift in her tone," she added when he gave her a puzzled look.

"That charm of yours is dangerously effective." Bree folded her arms on the table and leaned forward. "Because I still can't believe you talked me in to this trip."

"I'm still stunned by that one myself." Wes chuckled. "But I'm glad you agreed to join me. The trip wouldn't be nearly as fun solo."

Bree's mouth twisted in a reluctant smile. "Now that I'm here, I would think I've earned at least a preview of what to expect over this next week."

"All right." Wes leaned forward, holding back a grin. "We're having dinner tonight and we're going hiking in the morning."

"But where are we—"

"That's all I'm giving you." He held up a hand as the server approached their table with the sampler of appetizers he'd ordered. "I want you to be surprised, especially in Asheville. So you're going to have to give me a little leeway here."

Bree opened her mouth to object, but a genuine smile lit her eyes as she turned her attention to the chicken wings, fried green tomatoes and potato fritters.

"I shouldn't be eating any of this." She grabbed a saucer and unwrapped her silverware. "But that won't stop me from sampling every bit of it."

Wes grinned, reminding himself of all the reasons he shouldn't be attracted to her. His brain agreed, but his body and heart had gone rogue.

He wanted to spend more time with Bree. To learn everything there was to know about her. He couldn't stop the visions of her in his bed, calling his name.

Wes sighed softly. Giving himself the keep-it-in-your-pants speech wouldn't be enough. Brianna Evans had burrowed under his skin and was working her way into his heart.

Chapter 9

Bree stood in front of the mirror in her hotel room and smoothed down her skirt. So maybe the little black dress was sexier than anything she'd normally wear to a business meeting. And maybe she had made a real effort with her makeup tonight.

It wasn't as if she'd flirted with him.

Okay, maybe she had, but only a little. It was certainly nothing serious.

Her phone rang. It was a video call from Bex. Bree cringed. For a moment, she considered not answering, but that would've worried Bex more.

"Hey. You caught me on the way out to dinner." Bree tried to sound nonchalant.

"Obviously, you're not going for pizza and a beer down at the pub." Bex's expression grew wary, as did her tone. "Let me see what you're wearing."

Bree breathed out a long sigh and extended her arm, holding the phone up so Bex could take in the entire outfit—cleavage and all.

"So this is a date." Bex's tone had gone from wary to alarmed.

"It isn't a date." The objection felt weak, even to Bree. "There's a restaurant in our hotel, and it happens to have a dress code."

"Does that dress code require cleavage? The girls are looking pretty spectacular tonight."

Bree's cheeks stung with heat. She smoothed a hand down the clingy, black draped jersey dress. "You're the one who's always saying I don't show off my assets enough."

"And today is the day you decide to listen?" Bex sucked in a deep breath. "Look, Bree, we both know you *really* like this guy. Hell, I like the guy. In any other circumstance, I'd tell you to go for it. Have a little fun. But there are three really important things for you to remember. Wes doesn't want anything serious, you do and this guy is the one standing between us getting what we want out of the tournament. Don't forget any of that."

"You think I'm too naive to hold my own with Wes."

"It isn't that, and this isn't me scolding you or saying in any way that you should change who you are. You see the good in everyone and you wear your heart on your sleeve. I love those things about you. It's why we make such a good team. You balance out my craziness, and I need that." Bex smiled into the camera. "But for you, *nothing* is strictly business. I doubt Wes shares your philosophy."

Bex wasn't wrong. Bree was playing with fire and she knew it. Still, she was drawn to Wes in a way she couldn't explain. Like they were meant to be together. If not as lovers, at least as friends.

There was a knock at her hotel-room door. A knot tightened in her belly.

"I have to go." Bree lowered her voice. "But I'll remember what you've said. Promise."

"Fine. Have fun." Bex's exasperated tone indicated she knew her advice had fallen on deaf ears. "Just be careful. I don't want to have to come out there and kick his ass."

"'Bye, Bex." Bree ended the call and dropped the phone in her clutch. She surveyed herself in the mirror one last time.

This is business. Relax. Have fun.

It was a hollow claim, because the closer she got to the door, the faster her heart beat.

Bree opened the door. "You're early."

"And you...look amazing." Wes jammed his hands in his pockets and leaned against the doorway.

"You sound surprised." There was a nervous lilt to her laughter. "I'd like to think I cleaned up pretty well the night we met."

"You did, but tonight..." He sucked in a deep breath as he surveyed her from head to toe. "Let's just say you've turned it up a notch."

Brianna looked stunning in a form-fitting little black dress that was ultra-feminine and incredibly flattering on her body. The draped neckline drew his attention to her full breasts. The bow-tie belt detail highlighted her small waist and the clingy fabric hugged every single curve.

He cleared his throat as he took a cream-colored cashmere cardigan from her and helped her into it.

She tied the sash at her waist, grabbed her bag and stepped into the hall.

Wes followed her to the elevator, his eyes drawn to how the fabric hugged her curvy bottom. He dragged his eyes away and punched the down button for the elevator.

"You're going to love this restaurant." Wes stared at the elevator doors rather than looking at her. "And this is one of my favorite places to stay whenever I come here."

"It's a beautiful hotel, and it's right across the street from the Biltmore Estate." Bree ran her fingers through her shoulder-length curls. "Almost makes me wish we were going to be here a bit longer, so I'd have time to visit."

"Careful." He grinned inwardly, determined not to ruin the surprise he had planned for her the next day. "Almost sounds like you're enjoying your time with me."

"Don't get too cocky." She laughed. "It's too early to make that call, but so far…yes. I am enjoying the trip."

"Fair enough." He stepped off the elevator and offered his arm to her. She reluctantly slipped her arm through his and fell in step beside him.

They entered the restaurant, greeted by the enticing scent of savory, grilled meat. The gentle strains of live guitar music filled the air.

"It's like an upscale hunting lodge." Bree surveyed

the brown-and-red leather seating and the antler chandeliers hanging overhead. "I honestly wouldn't have thought that was possible."

Wes chuckled. "Wait until you taste the food."

"I've already studied the menu, so I know exactly what I want."

His gaze raked over Bree, his heart beating a little faster. He knew exactly what he wanted, too. But it would be better for both of them if he showed restraint.

They were shown to a table, then placed their orders, falling into an easy conversation about Asheville and some of the activities he enjoyed here.

"Tomorrow morning, I'll take you on a walking tour of downtown. It's called the Urban Trail." Wes sipped his beer.

"You've probably done the trail at least a half a dozen times."

"Actually, I've only done it once with my mother and aunt. Normally, when I come to town I prefer something a little more challenging. Like a brisk hike."

Bree raised an eyebrow, as if she'd been challenged. "Then let's do that instead."

"The hike takes about four hours."

"Then we should get started early."

"The trail can be pretty muddy and it's challenging for a beginner."

"Who says I'm a beginner?" Bree asked incredulously. "You do know I make my living as an athlete, right?"

"Fine." Wes raised his hands, giving in. Bree was determined to go hiking with him. Maybe they'd take the city walking tour later. "Then we'd better make it an early night."

He was disappointed by the prospect.

"Not necessarily." She shrugged. "I'm not in training right now. I can handle staying up past my bedtime. Unless you're the one who can't function without eight hours of beauty sleep."

"I'll manage. Got hiking clothes and shoes?"

"I do."

Bree for the win.

The server brought out his fried calamari and her roasted pear salad. The look of satisfaction on Bree's face after she took the first bite of her salad did things to him.

"Anything else I need to know about tomorrow?"

Wes dug in to his calamari and tried to shift his mind to something that didn't get him so hot and bothered. Like cold showers and sewer drains.

"We'll be on a tight schedule, and you'll want to wear comfortable and casual clothing and footwear for tomorrow afternoon."

"Okay." The expression on Bree's face indicated that the wheels in her head were turning. "Anything else?"

"No." Wes enjoyed keeping her in suspense. Something about her frustrated little pout made him want to kiss her. He wasn't sure who was torturing whom.

Later, as he dined on grass-fed filet mignon and she ate her pan-roasted duck breast, butternut squash risotto and bacon-braised greens, their conversation fell into a comfortable rhythm.

"You didn't mention what took your family to London." Bree sipped her wine.

"My mother was the house manager for a wealthy family that relocated to London," Wes said, then sighed. "Actually, that's what gave us the opportunity to move to London. The reason we moved is because my mother wanted a fresh start for all of us."

Bree's eyes were sympathetic and kind, like a warm hug from a dear friend. He could tell she wanted to delve deeper, but seemed unsure if she should.

"My parents divorced when my brother and I were kids. He was a jazz saxophonist who headlined his own band. He and my mom met when he hired her as the band's female vocalist."

"Your parents were musicians? They must've lived an exciting life." She sliced into her duck and took a bite.

"They did," Wes said. "Which is why the old man didn't adjust too well to family life and working in a factory. He stuck it out eight or nine years, but then he became restless.

"He got the band back together and snagged a few local gigs. At first, that was enough. But then he wanted to hit the road and tour again." Wes drained his beer, then signaled for another. "My mother didn't want to drag us all over the world, and she refused to leave us behind. She didn't want anyone else raising her kids—not even my grandmother."

"Is that when they split?"

"Not at first. He hired a new vocalist and his band toured the States, then Europe. His calls and postcards became less frequent. Eventually he sent a letter saying that he loved us, but that this was something he needed to do for himself. The divorce papers showed up not long afterward."

"Wes, I'm sorry." There was comfort and compassion in her voice, rather than pity. "I understand the betrayal you feel when a parent walks away from you like that…it's indescribable."

"I thought your parents were still together."

Bree seemed to carefully debate her next words. "I'm adopted."

Wes straightened in his seat, the hair lifting on the back of his neck. "You're adopted?"

"Yes." She seemed surprised by his reaction.

"I didn't mean for it to sound as if…" He took a breath. *Get it together, man.* "It's just that I've seen some of your interviews and pictures of your family. You resemble your mother quite a bit. I guess we see what we expect to see."

Nice save.

Bree's shoulders relaxed. "My adoptive mother is my biological great aunt. My bio mom had me when she was really young. Her aunt and uncle weren't able to conceive and they couldn't afford in vitro. So when they learned my bio mom was pregnant and didn't want the baby, they talked her out of termination and offered to adopt me. I got lucky twice."

"It's good you were able to stay with family." He assessed her carefully before asking his next question. Her open expression seemed to give him permission. "If you don't mind me asking, what's your relationship with your birth mom?"

"We don't have one," Bree responded matter-of-factly, but the light in her eyes dimmed and her smile lost its radiance.

Wes glided his hand across the table, wanting to touch hers. He wanted to give her the same comfort her smile had given him earlier. He froze, his fingers a few inches from Bree's.

Keep it strictly business. Maintain your distance.

"Sorry to hear that, Bree." He gripped his beer glass instead. "That must be hard."

"It's not that I don't see her. I do. At every family function. She went on with her life and became a successful lawyer. Got married. Had kids of her own." Bree forced a laugh. "And me, I'm this big family secret that everyone except her husband and kids know about."

Something deep in his chest bubbled, like hot lava threatening to spill out of a volcano. How could Bree's mother sit next to her at barbecues and family weddings, pretending they didn't share the strongest human bond? Didn't the woman have any idea how that must make Bree feel?

Wes tried to curb the anger building toward a woman he'd never even met. He'd always known how lucky he was to have his mother. She'd given up everything for him. Put all of her dreams aside to give him and his brother the best life she could. For that, he couldn't thank her enough.

But it was more than just Bree's situation that bothered him. Her revelation that she was adopted set all those wheels turning in his head. The ones that kept him awake at night.

Adopted children usually went to good homes. Better situations. What about the ones who didn't? Even when everything looked good from the outside, who could know what was happening behind closed doors?

Wes didn't realize neither of them had spoken in several minutes until her voice, soft and apologetic, broke through the jumble of thoughts that wrapped themselves around his skull and squeezed like a vise.

"I didn't mean to put a downer on this lovely meal. I'm not even sure why I told you that. I shouldn't have. Only a handful of people outside of my family know the truth. So, please don't tell anyone."

"Not my business to tell." He shrugged. "But I'm glad you felt comfortable enough to tell me."

Bree squirmed. Something in her eyes indicated that the ease she felt with him was a source of concern for her.

They had that in common, too.

As they finished dinner and shared a generous slice of pecan carrot cake, Wes tried to reassure himself that getting to know Bree was simply a team-building exercise designed to fortify their working relationship. But the truth gnawed at him.

He liked Bree. *A lot.*

He wanted her friendship, and a rogue part of his anatomy wanted something more.

Trying to strike the perfect balance between building an amicable, working relationship with Bree and keeping a safe emotional distance was a dangerous game. A lot was at stake. For him. For Bree. For Westbrook International.

He couldn't afford to screw this up.

Yet, when he walked her back to her room, he wasn't prepared to say good-night.

"Thank you for dinner." Bree leaned in, one hand pressed to his chest, and kissed his cheek. Her soft scent and body heat surrounded him.

He hadn't expected the innocent kiss or that he'd be overwhelmed by her nearness.

Bree's mouth lingered near his as she pulled away so slowly he could hear every microsecond ticking in his head. He willed himself to stay in control. To keep his hands shoved in his pockets, where they wouldn't get him into trouble.

"You're welcome." The words came out much quieter than he'd intended. He dropped his gaze to her sensual lips and she smiled.

"I'd ask you in for an after-dinner drink, but like you said, we've got an early morning." Her voice was soft and captivating, an unspoken invitation.

Wes wet his lower lip and tried to tear his attention away from her mouth and her soft gaze. Tried with every fiber of his being to ignore the fact that he wanted her desperately.

He couldn't.

Slipping his arms around her waist, he pulled her closer. His mouth inched toward hers. Bree's eyes drifted closed as she leaned in, closing the space that remained between them.

His lips were nearly on hers when laughter erupted from a loud group exiting the elevator. Startled, her eyes opened and she stepped beyond his grip.

Her cheeks were crimson and she somehow managed to look both surprised and disappointed.

Feelings he shared.

Still, another part of him was thankful. This was a business trip, not a love connection. Something they'd both do well to remember.

"Bree, I'm sorry, I—"

"Saved by the bell." She forced a smile, then dug her hotel key card out and bid him good-night before closing her door.

Wes dragged a hand through his hair and let out an exasperated sigh. He needed to pull it together or he and the project were in serious trouble.

Chapter 10

Bree hoisted on her backpack and made her way toward the sign that declared their arrival at the Looking Glass Rock Trail head in the Pisgah National Forest.

The forty-five-minute drive to the park had been filled with awkward silence over their near kiss the night before, something neither of them seemed willing to discuss.

She zipped her black jacket up to her neck to ward against the cool, brisk morning air. Bree secured her silk-lined knit hat, tugged on a pair of black gloves and wound a scarf around her neck.

The sun was up and the temperature was rising. By the time they'd hiked to the summit, she'd likely need to shed a few layers. But for now, her breath rose as a visible, steamy cloud in the air.

"Sure you're up for this?" Wes set the car alarm,

then zipped the keys in a backpack he'd stuffed with fruit, protein bars and several bottles of water. "The downtown walking tour is still an option."

"And miss climbing to the top of this…what did you call it again?" They'd seen the view of the commanding rock cliff from the other side. It was a rock climber's dream.

"Looking Glass Rock is a pluton monolith. It was formed when hot magma tried to push its way to the surface, but got stuck underground."

"How could it have been formed underground when it's nearly four thousand feet high?" She fastened the backpack straps that intersected her chest.

"A mountain once shielded the rock." Wes nodded toward the trail. "Over time, it wore away, leaving the igneous rock exposed."

Bree grinned. "Wouldn't have pegged you for a science nerd."

"I'm not." A pained look briefly marred Wesley's handsome face. He flashed an uneasy smile. "We'd better stretch, then get going. Got a full day ahead."

They stretched, then followed some steps. The trail opened onto a forest dominated by the towering trunks of dead hemlock trees. Because of the unseasonably warm weather, many of the newer species of trees that had taken root were in bloom, despite it being late winter.

The ground was dry and the gradual elevation of the trail made for a fairly easy hike. They climbed uphill beside a small stream, then the trail took a right and crossed the creek on a footbridge.

About a mile in, the ground changed from dirt to exposed rock.

Bree squatted down to touch the cool surface. "Can you believe this was once hot, molten liquid?"

"Pretty amazing when you think about it. This could've been an active volcano, spewing hot lava." Wes stepped closer, held out his hand and pulled Bree to her feet.

"Thanks." Bree's cheeks heated as her eyes met his. She tugged her hand free, then went ahead of him on the trail. Her pulse accelerated even more than it had from the exertion of the climb.

The trail rose in a series of hairpin turns, which made it possible to see the trail ahead and below. Switchbacks, Wes had called them. The switchbacks kept the trail from getting too steep.

Bree was thankful for the gradual increase. Despite being a runner and regular strength training, her thigh muscles burned in protest.

Along the way, Wes pointed out the flora and fauna. They'd seen cardinals, blue jays and ruby-throated hummingbirds, whose wings moved so rapidly they were a blur. Suddenly, a streak of white fur dashed across the trail.

"Was that a white squirrel?" Bree tried to pull out her phone and snap a picture, but the squirrel had zero interest in his fifteen minutes of fame.

"White squirrels are the unofficial mascot here in Brevard." Wes grinned. "There's a White Squirrel Festival here on Memorial Day weekend."

Bree scanned the forest, looking for the adorable little furry creature, hoping to snap a shot of it. It would look nice beside the photo of black squirrels she'd taken while visiting Toronto years earlier.

Wes handed her a bottle of water, and she accepted

it gratefully. Bree finished nearly half the bottle as she surveyed the area around them. It was peaceful and beautiful, despite the time of year.

"I see why you love coming here." Bree capped the bottle and stuffed it in her backpack.

"Not yet." He finished his bottle. "But you will. C'mon, we'd better keep moving."

Wes went ahead on the trail and she followed. Finally, they reached a helipad used to airlift injured climbers.

"Is this it?" She looked around. "There's no view here."

"Patience, grasshopper," he called over his shoulder, continuing ahead on a slightly downhill trail. Suddenly, the brush opened onto a rocky platform that offered a view of the valley below. "*This* is the money shot."

"It's incredible." She ventured forward carefully. There was no railing. Just a sheer rock cliff at the edge. "Is it safe?"

Wes tested the surface. "There's no ice and it's dry today, so it shouldn't be slippery. Stay on the flatter area bordering the forest and don't venture too close to the edge. It's a long way down."

Bree inched out farther, enjoying the gentle breeze and the sunshine, and she studied the remarkable view below.

"The view must be stunning when the trees are all green during summer, or in the fall when the leaves are changing colors."

"It is." There was a sadness behind Wes's smile that made her heart ache. "Maybe we'll get a chance to come back here when the tournament is over. Sort of a celebration climb."

"I like that idea." Bree returned her attention to the view, not wanting Wes to see how happy the thought made her. She snapped a few shots of the view with her phone, then pointed to a mountain in the distance. "What's that?"

"Black Balsam Knob and that's Pisgah Mountain." Wes pointed to a ridge with a succession of peaks.

Bree moved forward, taking photos, then suddenly lost her footing. She dropped her phone, but Wes caught it and her before either hit the ground.

"I've got you. You're okay." His voice was calm and reassuring as he steadied her. "You just slipped on a patch of algae."

"But if I'd… I mean, if you hadn't…" Her heart raced as she imagined what could've happened if Wes hadn't been there. She hugged him. "Thank you."

"I'd love to take credit for being the hero, but if you'd fallen, you would've only sustained a few cuts and bruises. I doubt you'd have sailed off the cliff. It's pretty flat here." He held her in his arms. "I'd never put you in jeopardy."

Bree leaned back and met his gaze. "Seriously, Wes, I appreciate what you did."

"I'm letting you go now, so watch your step." His smile reassured her. "Stand over there and I'll get a few shots of you with the mountains in the background."

He took a few photos with her phone, then handed it back to her, and she took a few of him in silly poses that made them both laugh and put her at ease.

"If you aren't a science geek, how do you know so

much about pluton monoliths and the kinds of trees up here?" Bree studied his face as a stormy cloud seemed to settle over him, making her regret the question.

"My dad." Wes frowned as he sat down and removed his backpack. He rummaged inside and pulled out an apple. He handed it to her before getting another for himself.

Bree took off her backpack and sat on the ground beside Wes. She nibbled on the apple, hoping Wes would tell her more, but not wanting to push him. The subject of his father was obviously a sensitive one.

"My dad had been on the road traveling with his band for several months. When he finally came home, I'd asked him to stay with us rather than going back out on the road." Wes chewed a bite of his apple.

"He didn't answer, but a couple days later, he brought me up here and showed me this incredible view." Wes looked around, staring off into the distance. "He said there was so much out there, and that he wanted to experience all of it. And he wanted the same for me, even if that took us on different paths."

Bree placed a hand on Wes's arm before she could stop herself. He seemed to find comfort in the gesture.

"Wes, I'm sorry about your dad." She lowered her voice, not wanting the hikers who'd joined them on the rocky cliff to overhear her. "Do you and your dad keep in touch?"

"Barely, but I'm fine with things the way they are." His expression belied his forceful statement, but Bree didn't press.

"What about your younger brother?"

"Drake sees our father as this larger-than-life heroic figure. He followed his footsteps and became a musician."

"Another sax player in the family?" Bree smiled, trying to lighten the mood.

"A drummer. He practiced on an old set of drums dad left behind."

"Your mom must've been a very patient woman."

"She was." Wes flashed a genuine smile that made her heart soar. "Guess it paid off. Drake's pretty good. He's been working as a session musician mostly, hoping to eventually start his own jazz trio."

"Excuse me," one of the hikers said. "Would you mind taking a group photo of our family?"

Wes obliged, climbing to his feet and accepting the young brunette's cell phone. He took a series of photos of their family of four before handing it back to her.

"Thanks." The girl beamed. "I'd be happy to take a few shots of you and your girl... Oh my God. Look, Mom! It's Bree Evans. It's so great to meet you. I'm a huge fan."

"Thank you so much. It's a pleasure to meet you, too." Bree grinned, hoping she didn't look like a sweaty, hot mess. "And thank you for offering to take our photo, but—"

"Yes," Wes interrupted. "We'd love for you to take some pictures of us."

Bree handed the girl her phone and she and Wes stood together on the rocky cliff with the trees in early bloom spread out behind them.

The girl frowned after taking the photo. "You both look uncomfortable in this one. Maybe we should try again. Stand a little closer and maybe try smiling."

Wes and Bree looked at each other and laughed,

stepping a little closer. He wrapped an arm around her and they smiled.

"Much better." The girl took a few more shots and smiled. She returned the phone and asked that Wes take photos of her and her family with Bree. After Bree autographed the girl's backpack, she and her family began their descent back down the trail.

"We'd better go, too." He picked up both backpacks and handed Bree hers. "There's one more thing I want to show you before we head back to the hotel."

Bree turned and looked one last time at the incredible view, wishing they could stay longer. Or maybe it was just her time with Wes that she didn't want to end.

Chapter 11

Wesley tapped softly on Bree's hotel-room door. She didn't answer right away.

He wouldn't blame her if she'd fallen asleep. After climbing Looking Glass Rock Trail and a quick drive to Looking Glass Falls, they'd grabbed fast food and returned to their respective rooms for a quick shower and change before heading out again.

Wes knocked again, louder this time.

"I'm ready." Bree rushed out of the door, filling the space between them with the scent of fresh summer peaches. Her hair, still wet from the shower, was pulled into a high ponytail.

She wore a casual dress in a bold handkerchief-style print. The vivid orange with accents of pink and teal suited Bree well. A nude leather belt cinched her waist. A tan jacket and nude ballet flats with an ankle strap completed the look.

Casual, but sexy. Funky, but not over the top.

"Something wrong?" Bree's gaze dropped to her feet. She flexed her leg, showing off a sexy, heart-shaped calf.

"Everything's good." Wes steered her down the hallway to the elevator.

The valet brought the car and they went just a little way up the street before he turned onto Biltmore Estate Drive.

"We're going to tour the house?" Bree's eyes lit up. She was clearly thrilled.

"Couldn't bring you to Asheville without taking you for a tour of the largest private residence and the most visited winery in America." Wes chuckled.

They parked and he opened her car door. His gaze instantly followed her mile-long legs to the hem of her dress, which ended well above her knees. Wes extended his hand to her, helping her out of the car. They made their way to the main house.

Wes had toured Biltmore before. But Bree's amazement as they toured the home, with its beautiful atrium, lavish furniture, extensive library and impressive grounds, made him feel he was seeing it all for the first time. There was something about her wide-eyed wonder and pure fascination with the estate that reminded him how genuine she was and how much he enjoyed being with her.

Maybe he wasn't a science nerd, but he was fascinated by history. It was the reason he'd visited the historic property, and several others all over the world, whenever his schedule permitted.

Bree squeezed his arm as she related her enchantment with the estate's incredible library of more than twenty-two thousand volumes.

"Relax, Belle," he teased. "There's a lot more to see."

His *Beauty and the Beast* reference wasn't lost on her. Bree pursed her lips and propped a fist on her hip.

"I happen to love that movie, and I know every single word to every single song. Call me Belle again and I'll start singing to the top of my lungs about the simplicity of this provincial life." She cocked an eyebrow that dared him to try her.

"You win." He couldn't help but grin. "Still, you can't deny the similari—"

Bree spread her arms and opened her mouth, preparing to go into song, when he wrapped his arms around her and pulled her closer.

They both dissolved into a fit of laughter that caused the people around them to give them odd looks.

"You were really going to do it, weren't you?" Wes asked, after they'd regained their composure and rejoined the tour.

"Would've been worth it to see the panicked look on your face." Bree wiped away tears from laughter. "Besides, I need to keep you on your toes. Can't be too predictable."

Wes chuckled. "Mission accomplished."

They toured the remainder of the house and the grounds together. After a tour of the winery, they sampled a variety of wines at the subsequent wine tasting, and purchased their favorites.

"Today was incredible." Bree's face practically

shone once they were in the car and heading down the long road that led off the Biltmore property. "Thank you."

"Glad you enjoyed it, but the night's not over. Got someplace special in mind for dinner. You'll love it."

"Let me pay this time," she said. "I know these are business expenses, but still… I should pick up the tab for something."

"You can pay when we get to Charlotte tomorrow." This wasn't a lovers' getaway, it was a business trip. Still, he didn't feel comfortable allowing Bree to pick up the tab for dinner tonight or any night.

"Deal," she conceded. "Where are we going?"

"You'll have to wait and see."

Bree agreed to his terms begrudgingly.

She should be annoyed with his little game. Yet, she'd been delighted by every one of his surprises. No reason to believe he'd disappoint her now.

Bree's belly tightened in a knot. Her anticipation over their mysterious dinner destination rose, along with a growing fondness for Wes.

They were working together as a team on a project that was equally important to their careers. They needed to get along so they could work together seamlessly.

Didn't her fondness for Wes make working together easier?

Bree focused on the scenery as they drove through the streets of the charming mountain town. She could keep telling herself this trip was strictly business. But her attraction to Wesley Adams was blooming like a pretty, but unwanted, weed.

She glanced at Wes. Was it possible he was growing more handsome as the day went on?

Bree wanted him. There was no doubt about that. He wanted her, too. She was equally sure of that. But did he see the potential for more between them? Did he want it the way she did?

"Everything okay? You've gotten really quiet."

"I'm thinking, that's all."

"Anything you want to talk about?"

"Not really."

"Fair enough." Wes was quiet for a moment, as if contemplating his next question. He seemed to ask despite his better judgment. "Then let me ask why making the tournament a family event is such a focal point for you?"

Discussing the tournament was exactly what she needed right now. After all, that was the point of the trip.

"The truth?" She turned to him. "Bex and I want to elevate the game. Pass our expertise on to the next generation of players. We're planning to put on volleyball clinics for kids eight to seventeen years old. Gearing the tournament toward families will allow us to tap in to our market."

"I see." He mulled over her revelation in silence for a moment. "It's a solid business idea. Who wouldn't want their kids to learn the sport from two of its most successful athletes? But in terms of the tournament, your target market doesn't align with the resort's."

"Pleasure Cove Luxury Resort isn't an adults-only destination," she countered.

"It isn't a family-friendly one, either. It's the kind

of place parents go to get away from their kids for a week."

"That's awful." She couldn't help laughing.

"It's also true." He chuckled, seemingly relieved the mood in the car had lightened. "That doesn't make them bad people. Let's face it, being a parent is one of the toughest jobs in the world. Sometimes you need to take a break and reset."

"You sound like a man who speaks from experience. Are there any little Wesleys out there I don't know about?" She grinned.

His shoulders seemed to stiffen and his smile vanished for a moment. He pulled up to the valet stand in front of a huge, pink stone building.

"No one out there is calling me Dad, I assure you." He forced a smile, but his eyes seemed sadder than she'd ever seen them. He nodded toward the building. "We're here."

A valet at the Omni Grove Park Inn opened the door and helped her out of the car. Wes handed him the keys.

"Shall we?" Wes waved a hand toward the entrance of the building.

"This building is amazing." Bree surveyed the open front hall, which had two massive stone fireplaces blazing. Most of the furniture was art deco. "How long has this place been here?"

"Over a hundred years. The exterior was hewn out of native granite. The roof is comprised of red clay tiles. Some of the original furniture is still on display throughout the hotel."

Wes led her to the Sunset Terrace—a steak-and-seafood restaurant situated on a large, covered outdoor terrace with an incredible mountain view. The server seated them.

"It's stunning." Bree was mesmerized by the incredible view of the mountains as the sun began to set. "A perfect end to a perfect day."

"I wanted your final night here to be memorable." Wes smiled sheepishly. He added quickly, "To give you a sense of the area."

"Then why do I feel like I'm on a date?" Bree couldn't help the smirk that slowly spread across her face.

His eyes widened and he coughed. Wes took a deep drink of his water without response.

"Or maybe I just need to get out more." She sipped her water then returned the glass to the table. "Because the last time I had this much fun was the night we spent together in London."

Wes seemed relieved when the server appeared and took their orders. By the time the man left, he'd gathered himself.

"Bree…" He said her name as if it'd taken every ounce of his energy to utter it. "I like you. A lot. And maybe you're right. This was supposed to be a simple business trip, but I've turned it into what feels like something *more*. It wasn't intentional."

"So we stumbled into a romantic getaway?" One eyebrow raised, she sipped her water.

"Maybe I allowed my attraction to you to shape my choices." Wes sighed heavily. "But the fact remains that we'll be working together, and we need to keep things professional."

"Not to mention that you're not in the market for

anything serious. *Ever.*" She buried her hurt behind a teasing tone and forced smile.

"Then there's that." Wes seemed saddened by the concession. He thanked the server for bringing their bread and decanting their wine. "I wish the circumstances were different."

"What makes you think I'm looking for more?" She traced the bottom of her wineglass, her gaze on her fingertips.

"Because you can't even look me in the eye when you ask the question." He was clearly amused. "Before I met you, I thought the good girl thing was an act to garner sponsorships. It isn't. That's who you genuinely are. That isn't a bad thing, Bree. But I don't want to be known as the scoundrel who broke the heart of America's volleyball sweetheart."

Bree met his gaze, resenting that he knew her so well. Maybe it was the beautiful, romantic setting, but she wasn't prepared to back down.

That night in London she'd been sure they'd connected. That there'd been the potential for something meaningful between them. The past two days had reinforced that belief.

Something was definitely there. Every moment they spent together indicated Wes felt the same.

What is he so afraid of?

They were attracted to each other. So why couldn't they just be adults about it?

Regardless of what happened between them personally, they could simply agree to maintain a professional working relationship.

Bree formulated a proposal in her head.

Sound confident, not desperate.

When she returned her gaze to his, he was carefully assessing her. There was a distance in his gaze that wasn't there moments before.

She lost her nerve, panic gripping her. What if Wes turned her down? Bree couldn't deal with another humiliating rejection.

"So about the tournament…" Wes leaned back in his chair. "I think we agree now that family-friendly isn't the way to go. But I promise to promote your volleyball clinics any way I can. After all, it's the kids' parents who'll be paying for it."

"True." He'd given her a small concession, likely out of pity. Still, she couldn't afford to turn down his offer. "We'd appreciate that."

"You'll need to have your camp dates, website, organization and promo in place by the time we start printing marketing materials. Think you can handle that?" He'd slipped back into business mode, as if their earlier conversation hadn't occurred.

If only Bree could be so pragmatic and detached.

"We'll be ready," she said resolutely. "Bex is restless. She'll be glad to have a project to take on."

"If you need help with the planning and promo—"

"You'd take on a project as small as ours?"

"For high-profile clients like you and Bex? Sure. But I'm not suggesting you hire me. I'm talking about helping as a friend."

"Friends…is that what we are, Wes?" The stunned expression on his face made her regret her words. Wes hadn't done anything wrong. Hadn't promised her anything more than this…whatever this may be. "Sorry. I shouldn't have said that. Your offer is generous. Thank you. I'll talk it over with Bex."

"The sun is setting." Wes pointed in the distance. He seemed anxious to change the subject.

The sky was streaked with lovely shades of purple and orange. The entire scene glowed like a luminescent oil painting.

"It's beautiful. I could sit here staring at it all day."

"Me, too." Wes wasn't looking at the sky. His gaze met hers for a moment that felt like an eternity before he finally turned to survey the mountain range in the distance.

Heart racing and hands trembling, Bree did the same, determined to ignore the mixed signals Wesley Adams was sending.

"Dinner was amazing. Thank you again for such a lovely evening." Bree stopped in front of her hotel-room door.

"It was a good day," Wes said softly, leaning against the door frame. His eyes met hers, and were filled with the same longing, desire and frustration she felt.

And those feelings were heightened, as they'd dined on a tower of lobster, shrimp, crab and oysters.

Bree sank her teeth into her lower lip, her heart racing. The idea had been brewing in her head all night, and she'd been emboldened by the longing in his eyes and the gruffness of his voice.

Even now, she could feel the gentle tug between them. So why couldn't she just say what they were obviously both thinking?

"Wes…" Bree reached out to straighten his tie. "I'm not ready for our night to end."

"We could grab dessert. Maybe go dancing—"

"No." She stepped closer, their eyes meeting. Her

heart beat faster. "I want you. Here. With me. I know you want that, too."

"I do." He sighed heavily. "But we've been over all the reasons this is a terrible idea. Nothing's changed." He pushed a few strands of hair from her face. "I don't want to hurt you, Bree. And I don't want to jeopardize the friendship we've been building."

"Neither do I." Her eyes met his, her voice soft. "And we won't." *Stay calm. Sound confident, not desperate.* "I don't expect anything more than tonight. No promises, no obligations. Just…us."

Bree slipped her arms around his waist, her gaze trained on his as she tried to read him, hoping he'd say yes.

Chapter 12

Wes was trying to do what was in Bree's best interest, but she wasn't making it easy.

Then again, neither had he. Dinner overlooking the sunset? What the hell was he thinking?

This trip was supposed to be about getting better acquainted with the State of North Carolina. Instead, they'd been reminded of all of the reasons they'd gotten on so well together that night in London. The reasons they seemed perfect together.

"I want you, Bree. You know that, but—"

"You're not looking for anything serious." Her tone was sexy, teasing. She leaned in closer. Her soft, sweet scent teased his nostrils. The heat radiating from her body raised his temperature. "Neither am I."

It was a lie, and they both knew it. A lie he wanted desperately to believe.

Wes gripped her shoulders, drowning in her soft gaze. Thoughts of Bree occupied every available space in his brain. Distracted him from what he should be focused on right now—the tournament.

And yet…he wanted this. He wanted her.

The thud of Wes's heartbeat grew louder, his desire for Bree building. He leaned down and slipped his fingers into her hair as his mouth met hers.

A soft sigh escaped her mouth as she pressed her hands to his back and pulled him closer, melding the warmth of her body to his. He pinned her against the door as he captured her mouth in an intense kiss that made him ache for her.

His tongue delved inside her warm mouth. She welcomed it. Glided her own tongue along his as she gripped his shirt.

The voice in his head that was screaming at him not to do this was drowned out by the thud of his heart, his raging pulse and his feverish desire for her.

The elevator dinged, interrupting them as it had the night before. Wes pulled himself away, his eyes studying hers. This time, he couldn't walk away. He extended his palm, his eyes not leaving hers.

Bree dug out her key card and placed it in his palm. There was a hardened edge to her expression, belied by the slight trembling of her hands and her shallow breathing. Wes ushered them inside her room and wrapped one arm around Bree's waist, tugging her body against his.

He trailed kisses down her neck, inhaling her enticing scent. He pressed a soft kiss to her earlobe, then whispered in her ear, "Mixing business and pleasure is always a risky move."

Bree slid one hand up his chest. Her eyes blazed with passion, desire and a bit of defiance. She had no intention of backing down. At this point, neither did he. "Don't worry. I'm worth it."

The edge of his mouth curled. It wasn't the response he'd expected, but it was a sentiment he shared.

She captured his mouth in a greedy kiss that allayed any doubts about whether this was what she truly wanted. About whether she could accept his terms for engagement.

Good. No more Mr. Nice Guy.

Wes lowered his hands to the swell of her curvy bottom, swallowing her soft murmur in response. His body ached with his need for her. A need that'd been simmering since the night they met in London. But now it was at a full-blown boil.

Bree was responsive to his touch as his hands glided along her body—a perfect blend of feminine curves and athletic muscle. Her desire was a living, breathing, palpable thing that demanded satisfaction. He wanted nothing more than to give it to her.

Though the past two days indicated otherwise, this wasn't a fairy-tale romance. Tonight was about passion and desire, mind-blowing sex and pure satisfaction. Then they would both move on.

Wes turned Bree around and nestled her bottom against him as he trailed kisses down her neck. He slipped her dress slightly off her shoulder, and continued kissing his way down it.

She grabbed the hem of her dress and lifted it, but he stopped her.

"Don't take it off." He growled, his lips brushing her ear. He palmed her breast, tracing the tight bud with his thumb. Wes glided his other hand down her side, then up the inside of her thigh. "All night I've imagined what it'd be like to bend you over in this little dress and take you from behind."

Wes slid his fingertips along the crease of her hip, then across the waistband of her silky underwear. Her nipple beaded as he slipped his hand beneath the elastic band and over the narrow patch of curls. Bree gasped when he stroked the stiff bundle of nerves.

"Damn, you're wet." He breathed in her ear, running his tongue along its outer shell. Wes flicked his finger over the nub, enjoying her small gasp and the way her belly tightened in response. "Been thinking about me, haven't you?"

"No longer than you've been thinking about me." The statement began with defiance, but ended with a sensual murmur that did things to him.

"You're right." Wes chuckled, pulling her tighter against his growing shaft. "Because I've been wanting to do this since the night we met."

Wes splayed two fingers and slipped them back and forth over the hardened nub. Bree sucked in a deep breath and looped an arm around his neck, her hips moving against his hand.

He slipped his other hand beneath her dress and gripped her waist, pulling her tight against him. His eyes drifted closed as he reveled in the delicious sensation of her moving against his shaft.

His mouth pressed to her ear, Wes whispered sweet, filthy nothings in it. She rode his hand, her movement growing frenzied as he related every dirty deed he had planned for their night together. Including how he planned to worship that world-champion body of hers with his tongue.

What was it about Bree Evans that made him crazy with want?

"Oh, my God, Wes." Bree was close. Her knees trembled. Her breath came in short, hard exhalations that made his already taut member hard as steel.

He'd wanted to take her from behind. Keep it impersonal. Like two strangers in the dark. But there was something about the way she said his name. Something about how she felt in his arms. He wanted to see every inch of her. To stare in her eyes while she shattered, his name on her tongue.

He gathered her in his arms and carried her to bed.

Bree's heart raced as Wesley set her on her feet beside the bed and started to remove his shirt, one painstaking button at a time.

"Thought we were keeping it quick and dirty." She'd been disappointed that he'd wanted to make their first time together feel impersonal. Transactional. But she thought she'd done a relatively good job of hiding it. After all, that's what she'd agreed to. A no-strings fling.

"Changed my mind." He tossed his shirt and removed his pants without offering further explanation, then growled in her ear, "Now take that dress off before I do."

"Sounds like fun." Bree couldn't help the grin that curled the edges of her mouth at the thought.

Even in the limited light of her darkened hotel room, she could see that she'd surprised him again.

She squealed when he lifted her and tossed her onto

the bed. Suddenly, the dress was off, he'd removed her bra and they were both down to their underwear. Wes trailed kisses down her chest and belly before slowly dragging her panties down her legs.

Before she could react, he'd pressed his open mouth between her legs, his tongue lapping at her sensitive clit. Bree moaned with pleasure at the incredible sensation, calling his name before she could stop herself.

He slid his large palms beneath her hips, gripping them and pulling her closer to his mouth as he pleasured her with his tongue. She writhed as the warm sensation of ecstasy built at her center and her legs started to shake.

Wes pulled away and rummaged on the floor, then she could hear the tearing of the foil packet and make out the silhouette of Wes sheathing himself in the dark. He gripped the base of his length and slowly glided inside of her.

Bree sank her teeth into her lower lip, reveling in the sensation of Wes entering her, inch by inch, until he was fully seated. She cursed, her fingertips pressed to the strong muscles of his back, her fingernails digging into his skin.

Wes held her gaze as he moved his hips. Slowly. Precisely. The friction he created with each thrust of his hips was both torturous and delicious. She arched her back, desperate to heighten the sensation.

Her breathing was rapid and shallow as the pleasure building rose to a crescendo. She came hard, her muscles tensing and her legs shaking as she dug her heels into the mattress and her fingernails into his skin.

The hard muscles of his back tensed as she called his name, her body writhing in ecstasy. His gaze intensified as he moved his hips harder and faster until he'd reached his own edge. Wes's body stiffened and he cursed, his breathing labored. He tumbled on the bed beside her, both of them struggling to catch their breath.

Neither of them spoke.

Finally, Bree turned on her side, facing him. This was her idea, so she should be the one to break the awkward silence.

"Wes, that was…" She pressed a hand to his warm chest as she forced her eyes to meet his. "Incredible."

The edge of his mouth curled in a soft smile as he cupped her cheek. "No, you were incredible." He pressed a kiss to her mouth.

Her racing heart slowed just a bit and her shoulders relaxed. His compliment seemed genuine. Maybe he had enjoyed it as much as she had. Wanted her with the same intensity with which she wanted him.

"I know you're worried that I can't handle casual, but I can."

"Have you ever been in a casual relationship before?" He gave her a knowing smile that indicated he already knew the answer to his question.

"No." Her cheeks heated as she remembered how he'd teased her earlier about being a good girl. "That doesn't mean I'm incapable of being in one. I just hadn't encountered the right opportunity…until now."

Wes pushed a strand of hair off her face. "I want to believe you."

"You can." She kissed his mouth, then trailed kisses down his chest. *Convey strength and confidence.* She looked up at him and smiled in a manner she hoped was seductive. "But by the time I'm done with you, you won't want to walk away from me."

"Maybe you're right." He stroked her hair. "But I will walk away, and I need to know that you'll be okay with that."

Bree swallowed her disappointment and forced a big smile. "Don't worry. I'm a big girl. I'll be fine."

She resumed kissing her way down his hard chest and his tight abs, reminding herself that they were only having a little fun. Enjoying each other's company. That she shouldn't be falling for Wesley Adams. And ignoring the fact that she already was.

Chapter 13

Bree studied Wesley's handsome face as he rubbed his stubbled chin. They sat at a little table by the window. The sunshine warmed them as they chatted over their lavish breakfast, ordered via room service.

Neither of them had wanted to leave her room. They'd barely wanted to leave her bed.

"This is good." Wes took a bite of his eggs Benedict. He cut and speared another bite and held it out to Bree. "You have to try it."

She smiled, but was still shy about what felt like such an intimate gesture. Even after everything they'd done last night.

Her eyes not meeting his, Bree tucked her hair behind her ear and leaned forward, allowing him to slip the forkful of food into her mouth.

"Mmm…" The rich, flavorful hollandaise sauce

melded with the flavors of the forest ham, spinach and tomato. Her eyes drifted closed as she savored the food. "That is good."

His eyes were dark and hooded when her gaze met his. As if he was reliving the sights and sounds of their night together.

Her cheeks filled with heat at the possibility. She tried to push the vision of them together in bed from her head.

"Try my fruit cup." She speared pieces of strawberry, blueberry and banana on her fork and held it out to him.

Wes accepted the offering, his gaze still on her, as if he was waiting for her to say something.

"So, about last night." She dragged the words out slowly as she surveyed his expression.

"Last night was amazing." He sipped his double espresso, his gaze locked with hers.

"It was," Bree agreed, her cheeks stinging. She dropped her gaze as she sipped her decadent mocha cafe. "And I know you planned this spectacular trip for us, but I'd love it if we just…spent the day here in bed."

She laughed nervously in response to his stunned expression. "Don't worry, I'm not suggesting that this means anything. I'm just saying that I enjoyed our night together and I can't think of a better way to spend the day."

Wes set his mug on the table and shifted in his seat. He tilted his head slightly. "Sounds fantastic, but—"

"The rules we established last night still apply." Bree forced a grin, burying the hurt that simmered in her chest. Last night hadn't changed his feelings. "You made that crystal clear."

It was unlike her to be so forward. She'd been the shy wallflower who spent most of her school dances hovering in the corner, hoping not to be noticed. But there was something about Wesley Adams that eased her inhibitions.

Something deeper brewed between them, whether Wes acknowledged it or not.

"Now that that's all settled…" Bree strolled over to Wes and straddled his lap, her arms wrapped around his neck.

Wes chuckled as he wrapped his arms around her waist. "Who knew that America's volleyball sweetheart is a tempting seductress?"

"Not my usual MO." She shrugged. "But then my life usually doesn't leave much time for…this."

"Then I guess that makes me special." There was an uneasiness beneath his smile.

"Don't flatter yourself, playboy." She forced a grin. "I just happen to have some time on my hands."

Wes laughed heartily. He seemed to relax for the first time since they'd begun this conversation. "Then I guess I'm just lucky. Like the night we met."

Something about his statement—that he was lucky to have met her—warmed her chest and made her feel things she shouldn't about Wesley Adams. Feelings she should best ignore.

She kissed him and concentrated on all of the things she should be feeling. His hardened shaft pressed to her sensitive clit. The tightening of her beaded nipples, pressed against the hard muscles of his chest. The graze of his whiskers against her skin. The heat rising between them and the electricity that danced along her spine.

Bree wrapped her long legs around his waist as Wes carried her to the bedroom. He made love to her, and she lost herself in the heat and passion between them. In all of the physical sensations that it was safe to allow herself to feel. While ignoring the nagging insistence that, regardless of what either of them claimed, this was the beginning of something more.

Wes strode back to bed and sipped his beer as he watched Brianna sleeping. He should've returned to his own room last night. Maintained some space between them. But he hadn't. And since they'd chosen to stay another day, they'd only reserved one room. So tonight he had no room to which he could retreat.

He turned on the television with the volume low and studied Bree in the flickering television light. Her hair, loosened from the ponytail and still damp from their earlier shower, was everywhere. Mouth open, one foot hanging off the bed, makeup ruined, and still she was adorable. Probably as much a product of his unsettling feelings for her as her natural beauty.

Bree rolled over, throwing an arm across him. Wes sighed softly and slipped his arm beneath her head, cradling her against him. He stared at the ceiling, listening to the sound of her breathing, and hoped this wasn't a mistake they'd both regret in the weeks ahead.

His phone vibrated on the nightstand beside him. *Drake.* It was late for his brother to be calling. After sunset, Drake was usually preoccupied with a gig or a groupie he'd met during said gig.

"Isn't this the time of night vampires usually hunt their prey?" Wes smirked, teasing his younger brother.

"Usually. But we make an exception when our mothers stumble and fall down half a flight of stairs."

"What happened? Is she all right?" Wes slid his arm from beneath Brianna and climbed out of bed, pacing the floor near the window.

"She got tangled up in the bedding she was carrying downstairs to the wash. Damn lucky to have only have fractured her ankle and sprained her wrist." Drake's gravelly voice was that of a man who spent his nights in smoke-filled clubs.

Wes cursed, running a hand over his head. "This happened tonight?"

Drake hesitated before responding. "Last night. We've been trying to reach you, but your phone was off."

"My phone died last night. I've been…preoccupied." Wes glanced back at Bree. "Started charging it about an hour ago."

He'd always been the reliable son. The one who'd drop everything to help out his mother. But he'd failed her when she'd needed him most, a mistake he wouldn't make again.

"Thanks for being there, Drake."

"She's my mother, too." His words were laced with resentment. "Maybe I'm not always there physically, but I do whatever I can for Mom, no matter where I am in the world."

"Didn't mean to imply otherwise. Like I said, I'm just glad you were able to be there." Wes sighed, kneading the tension in his neck. "Is she still at the hospital?"

"Yes. Her doctor wants to hold her one more night for observation, in light of her Parkinson's." His brother cleared his throat. "When do you think you can get here? I'd love to stay, but I have to catch a plane in the morning. The band's got a gig in Germany in a few days."

"I'm in Asheville, but I'll leave first thing in the morning. I'll be there tomorrow afternoon. Is Mama awake? Can I talk to her?"

"She's resting. The pain meds knocked her out. I'll be leaving shortly, but between Aunt May, Dallas and Shay, she's in good hands. So don't worry. And Wes…" Drake's tone had softened, the tension gone.

"Yeah?"

"Don't beat yourself up over this. There's nothing you could've done to prevent this. And no one blames you for taking a little time for yourself. Certainly not Mama."

Wes wouldn't commit to not feeling guilty about allowing himself to be distracted when there was so much on the line professionally and personally. Still, he appreciated his brother's assurance.

Chapter 14

Bree awoke just in time to see Wesley striding out of the bathroom, freshly showered, with a towel slung low across his waist. As he bent over his luggage, the beads of water on his brown skin highlighted the strong muscles of his shoulders and back.

"Good morning." She sat up in bed, pulling the cover up around her.

"You're up. Good." He turned to her, a grave expression tugging down the corners of his mouth. "I'm afraid I have to bail on the rest of our trip. I have a family emergency. I need to be back home in New Bern as soon as possible."

"What happened? Is it your mother?" Panic bloomed in Bree's chest on his behalf. She knew how close they were.

"My mother tripped down the stairs. She fractured

her ankle and sprained her wrist. I know the injuries might seem minor, but I'm afraid it's part of a larger problem." He paused as if there was something more he wanted to say. Something he wasn't comfortable sharing with her. Wes sighed. "She was diagnosed with Parkinson's six months ago. I only learned about the diagnosis when I went to visit her after our first meeting about the tournament."

"That's where you spent the night." Bree's cheeks warmed the moment she blurted out the words.

"I stayed to accompany her to the doctor the next day and to help out around the house." A knowing smirk curled the corner of Wes's mouth.

"Sorry to hear about your mother. About the fall and the diagnosis." Bree forced her eyes to meet his rather than take in the brown skin stretched over his muscles. "I'll jump in the shower so we can get out of here as soon as possible."

"I'd appreciate that." He rummaged in his suitcase and produced a pair of jeans and a T-shirt. "And I hope you don't mind me stopping by the hospital to get my mom and then getting her settled at her place. As soon as I'm done, I'll get you back to Pleasure Cove."

"Of course not." She wasn't Wes's girlfriend, so why did she feel uneasy about meeting his mother? He'd probably introduce her as a friend or a business associate.

In little more than half an hour, she'd showered, dressed and tossed everything back into her suitcase. They ordered breakfast sandwiches to go and piled in the car.

"So your mom fell last night?" Bree asked between bites of her breakfast croissant.

Wes frowned and sipped his coffee, returning it to the cup holder before responding. "She fell the night before. My phone was off. My brother was finally able to reach me last night, after you'd gone to sleep."

"Oh." She nibbled on more of her sandwich. "So that's why you're…distant this morning. I'm the reason you missed the call about your mother."

"It's my fault. No one else's. Between my mother and the tournament… I should've made sure my phone was on. That I was available." Wesley narrowed his gaze, his eyes focused on the road and his jaw tight. She'd definitely struck a nerve.

"So maybe it isn't my fault directly, but it was me that distracted you." Bree echoed the sentiment clearly written on Wesley's face and implied by his words. "I'm sorry about that. If I'd known your mother was ill—"

"It wasn't your business to know. I only told you because…" He sighed, then muttered under his breath. "Don't really know why I told you. So I'd appreciate it if you wouldn't mention it to her when you meet her."

"Of course." Bree nodded, staring out the window. Hoping to hide the deep flush in her cheeks.

Wes was silent for a moment, his tone lower and softer when he spoke again. "Just so we're clear, I'll be introducing you as my friend and business associate."

"That's accurate. The business-associate part, I mean. The friendship…that's still a work-in-progress."

Wes chuckled. "I guess it is."

Bree clutched a vase of flowers as she approached Mrs. Adams's hospital room. She'd suggested that Wes go up ahead of her and make sure his mother was up to meeting someone new. She tapped on the partially open door, her heart racing. Bree stepped inside when a voice called for her to come inside.

"You must be Brianna." A wide grin spread across the woman's face. She was a beautiful older woman who seemed far too young to be Wesley's mother. "I'm Lena Adams. Wes stepped out to talk to someone about finally letting me out of this place. He told me to expect you. He didn't say you'd be bearing gifts."

Bree sighed in relief. The woman's warm, welcoming demeanor put her at ease. "I walked past the gift shop and they were so beautiful. I couldn't resist. I hope you like them."

"Like them? Honey, this bouquet is stunning. How thoughtful. Thank you." She accepted the crystal vase and inhaled the flowers before setting them on the nightstand beside her bed. She indicated a nearby chair. "Please, have a seat."

Bree sat in the chair, suddenly conscious of whether Mrs. Adams would think her blouse was cut too low or her jeans were too tight.

Relax. You're not his girlfriend.

"Speaking of beauty, you're even more stunning in person." Mrs. Adams grinned.

"Thank you." Bree's cheeks warmed. "Do you follow beach volleyball, Mrs. Adams?"

"Only during the Olympics. But I've seen you in at least a dozen commercials over the years." Excitement lit the older woman's eyes. "And call me Lena, please."

"Someone will be along shortly to complete your discharge." Wesley's tall frame filled the doorway. His eyes met Bree's for a moment before he turned them back to his mother. "I see you've met Bree."

"I have. You didn't tell me that she was as sweet as she is beautiful. Look what she brought me." Lena nodded toward the flowers.

"Thank you, Bree." Wes studied the expensive flower arrangement, then turned toward her. His expression was a mixture of gratitude and suspicion. "They're lovely."

Bree clasped her hands, her eyes roaming anywhere in the room except Wesley or his mother. The elegant bouquet of red roses and orange Asiatic lilies was an expensive gift to a woman she'd never met. But they were beautiful and Wes had said how much his mother enjoyed gardening. So she thought Lena would appreciate them. She hadn't given any thought to the message her gift was sending...until now.

"Yes, they are." Lena emphasized the words as she eyed her son sternly. She returned her warm grin to Bree. "I hope you'll join us at the house for lunch, Brianna. It won't take me long to throw something together. We'll just need to make a quick stop at the grocery store." She turned to Wes.

He frowned, his arms crossed. "The doctor made it very clear that you should get some rest and stay off your feet as much as possible."

"Relax. It'll be fine." She squeezed his arm, then turned to her. "Brianna?"

"I'd love to join you for lunch, but Wes is right. You should be resting. So why don't you let me fix lunch for you?"

Lena's eyes lit up and her smile widened. "That's so thoughtful, Brianna. But I can imagine how busy you must be. I don't want to be any trouble."

"It's no trouble at all. It'd be my pleasure."

"Then we have a date."

The attendant arrived and helped Lena into a wheelchair. They followed the attendant down the hall as he pushed Wes's mother and they chatted.

"Look, Bree, I appreciate your willingness to come here and the flowers…but you don't have to fix lunch. I can pick up something that's already prepared." His voice was hushed.

"Are you afraid to eat my cooking?" Bree teased, hoping to lighten his mood.

Wes held back a smirk. "Should I be?"

"Probably." Bree smiled. "Actual cooking isn't my gift. But, I can assemble a mean chicken salad. Don't worry. I'll pick up a rotisserie at the grocery store."

"Bree." He grabbed her arm, stopping her, so that their eyes met. Wes sighed. "I just want to make sure you understand that nothing has changed between us. We're still just business associates and friends—"

"With benefits." Bree narrowed her gaze, her chin tipped so her eyes met his. "You were crystal clear about that. I'm not an idiot, and I'm not trying to get to you through your mother—if that's what you're thinking."

Wes's stare signaled that he didn't buy her story.

"I got the flowers because they were pretty. I thought your mother would like them. I offered to make lunch because it was clear that if I didn't, she was going to insist on making lunch for us. And because she seems sweet. And I like her. But if you don't want me to have lunch with your mother, fine. I'll rent a car and head back."

"No. Don't. I'm sorry. I'm usually not so ungrateful. I swear." Wes rubbed the back of his neck. "Thank you for the flowers and for offering to make lunch. Maybe you can distract her while I move her bed downstairs. Otherwise, she'd insist on helping me."

Bree nodded and fell back in step with Wes as they caught up with the attendant and his mother.

Her cheeks flamed and a knot tightened in her gut. She hadn't been completely honest with Wesley. She wasn't actively pursuing Wes through his mother, but she wanted very much for Lena Adams to like her.

Wes finished the last bite of his second helping of Bree's cranberry-walnut chicken salad served on warm, fresh, buttery croissants from the local bakery. So maybe Bree couldn't cook, but she could *assemble* a damn tasty meal.

He'd wanted to get started on rearranging the house while Bree fixed lunch, but his mother had insisted he sit down with them until his cousin Dallas could come over and give him a hand with moving her bed. Though she didn't much like the idea of moving her bed downstairs, even temporarily.

"I know you're worried, son, but I still think you're making too big of a deal about this. I fell. Accidents happen. I'll be more careful from now on."

"You can't trudge up and down those steps in an air cast." He lowered his voice. "Not in your condition."

"I was recently diagnosed with Parkinson's," his mother explained to Bree, then turned her attention back to him. "There's a banister. Besides, it's not as if I can't put any pressure on the foot. And I need my stuff. You don't plan to bring my entire bedroom down, do you?"

Bree excused herself and left the kitchen as he and

his mother continued to debate the topic. It was one argument Lena Adams wouldn't win. She was going to sleep on the ground floor, whether she liked it or not.

"Excuse me." Bree returned a few minutes later, smiling. "But I think I might have a solution that'll satisfy you both."

"I'm all ears." His mother gave Bree her attention.

"By all means." Wes gestured for her to continue.

She asked them to follow her to the front of the house.

"Your kitchen has ample eating space, but you also have a formal dining room, which it seems you don't use much." Bree indicated the piles of papers and books that had accumulated on his mother's table again since his last cleaning.

"Point taken." His mother chuckled. "Go on."

"Well, it's such a lovely space. It's a shame you don't get more use out of it. The room is spacious and the pretty bay window faces that lovely little park across the street."

His mother nodded thoughtfully. "It's a sizable room and it does have a beautiful view. But it doesn't have a door and it's right at the entrance. Visitors will have full view of my bedroom."

"That's a simple fix." Bree's eyes lit up. "You could add a wall here and put in a door."

"What happens if she decides to sell the house? Not everyone will want a first-floor bedroom in lieu of a formal dining room." Wes appreciated what Bree was trying to do, but he had to be practical. He wanted his mother to be comfortable, but they couldn't ruin the resale value of the house.

"A valid point." Bree tilted her head, her chin resting on her fist for a moment. She snapped her fingers. "Add a pretty set of French doors instead of a traditional door."

"Guests would still be able to see into my bedroom."

"Not if you mount thick curtains on the door." Bree's gaze shifted from his mother, then to him, and back again.

A wide smile spread across his mother's face, her eyes dancing. "That's a brilliant idea, Brianna. My nephew Dallas is a contractor. He mentioned yesterday that the job they were supposed to work on for the next few days got rescheduled. Maybe he can squeeze me in. He'll be here soon, but I'm going to call him now, so he can give his crew plenty of notice. Besides, I don't want him to give someone else my spot."

"You object?" Bree asked when his mother left the room.

"No. Seems you have everything figured out."

"Why do I have the feeling we're not talking about the plans to relocate your mother's bedroom anymore?" Bree stepped closer.

Her sweet, citrusy scent—like mandarin oranges and orange blossoms—filled his nostrils. The two nights they'd spent together in Asheville rushed to mind with a vivid clarity. A knot tightened low in his belly. His heartbeat quickened and his temperature rose as he recalled the way her brown skin glowed in the moonlight. It took every ounce of willpower he could muster to refrain from leaning down and kissing her soft, glossy lips.

Bree seemed to relish her power over him, and the

fact that with his mother just a few feet away, he was forced to keep his hands to himself.

Pure torture.

"Dallas says he can have his crew here in the morning." His mother returned, saving him from the need to respond to Bree's statement. "He'll be here soon to take measurements. The job should only take a couple of days."

"We still need to move your bed downstairs for now." Wes folded his arms.

"Not necessary. I can sleep right here." His mother patted the sofa she was seated on.

"That thing is hard as a rock. I know." Wes clutched his back as he remembered the last time he'd crammed his long frame onto the uncomfortable pull-out sofa.

"I'm half a foot shorter than you, so I think I'll be all right." She held up her open hand when Wes objected. "This is my compromise. Take it or leave it."

"Fine." Wes blew out an exasperated breath. "But don't complain when your back muscles are as stiff as bricks."

"Deal." She indicated that he should kiss her on the cheek.

He did, then sat beside her, draping an arm over her shoulder. "You've eaten and Dallas will be here shortly. This is a good time for me to take Bree back to Pleasure Cove."

"What a shame." His mother frowned. "I was hoping she'd be here to see the finished result of her idea. Besides, I could use her help decorating the new room."

"Bree's a busy woman. She doesn't have time to

hang out here and play interior decorator." Wesley's shoulders tensed.

"Actually, since the rest of our trip is canceled, I don't have anything planned for the next couple of days." Bree smiled at his mother, her eyes not meeting his. "I'd love to help."

Wes turned to his mother, who was as excited as a kid at Christmas. If it made his mom happy and Bree didn't object, why should he?

They'd shared a bed for two nights. Surely he could deal with her being at his mother's house for two days.

"You sure about this?" Wes gave Bree one last out.

"Positive." Bree grinned. "This will be fun."

Between his mother and Bree, Wes didn't stand a chance.

Chapter 15

Lena Adams was an indomitable spitfire who wouldn't allow minor inconveniences like a fractured ankle or a sprained wrist to keep her from cooking a full meal for her guests. Bree was sure that if she hadn't insisted on helping the woman, Lena would've soldiered through the entire process herself.

She admired Lena's drive and determination, traits her son had obviously inherited.

In the course of an afternoon helping Lena prepare a three-course meal, Bree had doubled her cooking repertoire.

Bree stole another glance out of the kitchen window at Wes working in his mother's backyard. It was the end of winter, yet the North Carolina sunshine beat down overhead, making the already mild temperature feel considerably warmer. Wes had stripped off his T-shirt. The deep brown skin of his bare back and chest glistened with sweat. His black athletic shorts hung low on his hips.

Bree swallowed hard, then sunk her teeth into her lower lip. Her cheeks warmed and a sudden burst of heat crept down her torso and sank low in her belly.

Lena chuckled.

Shaken from her temporary haze, Bree returned to her work of dicing more potatoes for the potato salad.

"Business associates, eh?" The woman could hardly hold back her laughter. "Is that what they're calling it these days?"

Bree froze for a moment, unsure how to answer her.

"Don't know whether you two are trying to pull the wool over my eyes or your own, but in either case, it ain't working."

"I hate to disappoint you, Ms. Lena." Bree emptied the rest of the diced potatoes in a pot of water on the stove, then washed her hands. "But we really are business associates and friends."

"I hope that isn't true." Lena had a sad smile as she poured two icy glasses of syrupy sweet tea. She handed them to Bree. "It's obvious to anyone with one eye and half a brain that you two are into each other."

"Wes isn't looking for a relationship. He's made that abundantly clear." Bree's gaze drifted back to Wes outside. "Neither am I."

"Sometimes we don't know what we want until the situation presents itself." Lena nodded toward Wes. "My boys mean everything to me. But before Wes came along, I was set on a very different life. One that didn't include children or a stable home. I was terribly wrong because being their mother is the best thing that's ever happened to me."

Bree's chest ached and tears stung her eyes. It was clear why Wes loved his mother so much.

"I wish my birth mother felt the same way about me." Bree said the words before she could stop herself.

Her adoptive mother loved her with all her heart. She was grateful for that. Still, she couldn't shake the deep-rooted pain over her birth mother's inability to muster the slightest maternal affection toward her. The woman had two other children, whom she doted on, so clearly she possessed the capacity for maternal feelings. Evidently, Bree wasn't worthy of them.

"If she doesn't, she's either misguided or a fool." Lena squeezed Bree's arm. The woman's words were filled with indignation, but her tone and expression were filled with compassion. "Any woman would be grateful to have a daughter as kind and thoughtful as you."

Bree blinked back tears as she forced a smile. "Thanks."

Lena glanced out at Wes again. "He's probably dehydrated and doesn't even realize it. He gets so focused on the task ahead of him that he sometimes forgets how important it is to stop and take care of himself."

She dipped a towel into a bowl of icy water, wrung it, then draped the cool cloth over Bree's arm. Lena propped open the screen door and nodded toward Wes.

Bree made her way to the garden, where Wes had been working for the past few hours.

"Your mom thought you might like these." She handed him a glass of sweet tea and the cool towel.

He thanked her, then mopped his brow with the towel before hanging it around his neck and nearly draining the glass of tea.

"Your mom was worried you might be getting dehydrated. I can get another glass, if you'd like." She turned to go back to the house, but Wes caught her elbow.

"Thank you. For everything." He stared at her with a heated gaze that lit a flame inside of her and caused her breath to come in quick, shallow bursts. "I know you have better things to do with your time, but you've been great with my mom. I can't tell you how much I appreciate that."

"I'm enjoying my time with her. Besides, she's taught me a lot today." Bree glanced over her shoulder toward the house and saw the kitchen curtains stir. She eased her arm from his grip and took a step back.

"What's wrong?" Wes narrowed his gaze.

"Your mom is convinced there's something going on between us. I don't want to add fuel to the fire." She took a sip of her tea.

"I'll bet." Wes chuckled. "My mother seems genuinely taken with you, and she isn't an easy woman to impress."

"She doesn't strike me as a volleyball fan."

"It's not about what you do. If she's impressed, it's because of who you are. For her, it's all about character. The person you are when no one else is around." Wes frowned, his voice fading at the end.

Bree wanted to ask him if he was all right, but before she could he'd thrust his empty glass into her outstretched hand.

"It was kind of you to offer to stay tonight, but I

really don't mind taking you back to Pleasure Cove. And don't worry about my mother, she'll understand. I promise."

"No." Bree shook her head, then smiled. "I'm enjoying my time with her. And you." Her eyes met his heated stare. "I want to stay. Unless it's uncomfortable for you. My being here, I mean."

Wes leaned against the metal rake, still sizing her up, but not responding right away. The awkward silence stretched on between them for what felt like forever before he finally shrugged. "It's…different. Been a while since I brought a girl home. For any reason. So I'm not surprised that my mother is trying to make something bigger out of this. I hope she hasn't made you uncomfortable."

"No, of course not." Bree forced a smile, not wanting to reveal her discomfort at Wesley's words.

Wes tried to ignore the sound of the shower running in the Jack-and-Jill bathroom between his room and the guest room Bree would be sleeping in. Tried to ignore the vision of water sluicing down Bree's back, between her firm breasts and into the valley between her long legs.

He tried, but failed miserably. His body ached with want and left him with an unsettled feeling in his chest.

He wanted her. In a way that made it clear that what he craved was more than just her body. No matter how many times he tried to tell himself otherwise.

"Wes?" There was a knock at the bathroom door that led to his room.

He cleared his throat and edged closer to the door.

"I hate to bother you, but I can't find another towel."

"Sorry about that." Wes groaned. He meant to re-stock the towels after he'd taken his shower earlier. "I'll get you one."

Wes retrieved some towels from the hallway linen closet and returned to the door. He took a deep breath before he knocked. "Got them."

Bree cracked open the door slightly. The room was still filled with steam and her hair hung in wet curls that clung to her face.

"Thank you." She reached one arm out while shielding her body with the door. "I'll be out in a second, if you need to get in here."

"All I want is you." His gaze held hers. "Naked. In my bed."

Her eyes widened with surprise. She closed the door and bustled around the bathroom, but still hadn't answered him.

Wes groaned, his forehead pressed to the bathroom door. Brianna had gotten under his skin in a way no other woman had. Maybe it was good she hadn't accepted his proposition. She was saving him from himself.

Suddenly, the door opened and she stood before him in one of the fuzzy, cream-colored towels he'd just given her. She gave him a shy smile, but heat raged in her brown eyes.

"I believe you invited me to your room. Does the offer still stand?" Bree seemed to enjoy the stunned look on his face.

He didn't speak. Didn't nod. Instead, he leaned down, cradled her head and pressed his mouth to hers.

Slipped his tongue inside her warm, minty mouth. Pressed his body against hers.

Bree wrapped her arms around him, her hands pressed to his back as she murmured softly, her head tilted.

Her skin was soft and warm and she smelled sweet and sensual. He wanted to taste every inch of her heated skin. Make love to her until they were both sweaty, exhausted and fully satisfied.

Wes slid his hands to her back, then down to her bottom, pulling her against him. He let out a soft sigh at the intense pleasure of her wet heat pressed against him there. He slid his hands beneath the towel, gripped her naked flesh before he lifted her into his arms and carried her to his bed.

Bree's smile was hesitant. Filled with want and need. And something more. Something that tugged at his chest and felt oddly familiar.

He didn't have time to ruminate over it. She took his face into her hands and pulled his mouth down to hers. Kissed him slow and sweet in a way that revved up his body and ignited a flame deep in his chest. It was a feeling that could only mean trouble for both of them.

Wes stripped Bree of her towel and shed his T-shirt and boxers. He trailed kisses from her neck to her center, wet and glistening. Tasted her there. Lapped at her with his tongue while teasing her with his fingers. Until she shattered, her knees trembling and her lips pressed together to muffle her whimpers.

He kissed his way back up to her belly. Laved her hardened, beaded nipples as he slid inside her and rocked them both into a delicious abandon that made him want to forget everything but her.

"You're an incredible woman, Brianna Evans. In every way." Wes kissed her damp forehead and held her tight against him. "Thank you."

Bree was silent for a moment before she pressed a hand to his chest and lifted her head so her eyes met his. "Thank you for what?"

"For being here with me." Wes pulled the damp, curly strands of hair back and tucked them behind her ear so he could study her elegant features in the moonlight. He kissed her cheek. "For being so kind and thoughtful to my mother."

She smiled softly. "Thank you for letting me meet her. I know that isn't something you usually do."

He chuckled. "Try never."

"Why?" Bree hesitated before continuing. "Most guys who feel that way…to be honest, they're probably doing womankind a favor by not getting deeply involved with anyone. But you aren't like that. You're a genuinely good man. You deserve to be happy. To have a full life. So why are you so dead set against getting involved?"

Wes sighed heavily, folding one arm behind his head as he stared at the ceiling. "The men in my family haven't had a very good track record of being good mates."

"My mother gave me up at birth and hasn't wanted anything to do with me since." Bree shrugged, resting her chin on his chest. "Doesn't mean I'd do the same to my kid. Besides, we aren't our parents, Wes. Who we are is based on the decisions we make every single day. Like you making the choice to be there for your mother as she battles her illness. That's why this tournament is so important to you, isn't it?"

"Yes." He traced her bare shoulder with his calloused fingertips. "And I'm not basing my decision on parental history alone."

"We all make mistakes, Wes." Bree was quiet for a moment when he didn't respond. "Doesn't mean that's who we are or that we don't deserve happiness. What matters is that we try to rectify our mistakes and that we learn from them."

"A caged bird escaping its gilded cage." Her gaze dropped to the tattoo on the left side of his chest. The bird was designed of sheets of musical notes. The door it escaped looked like facing capital letter Gs. She traced the ink lightly with her fingertips. "Is that you?"

"No. Got it not long after I graduated university as sort of a tribute to my mother."

"You hoped your mother would go after her dreams again, once you and your brother were no longer her responsibility. That's sweet. *You're* sweet." She leaned in and kissed his mouth.

"But you shouldn't feel guilty about your mom missing out on the life she might've had. You should see the glow on her face when she talks about you and your brother. She doesn't seem to regret a moment of her life. I can't imagine she'd want you lugging around this burden of guilt on her behalf." Bree studied his face, waiting for his reaction.

It was a weight he'd been carrying for years. One not easily budged. He met her gaze. "This is who I am, Bree. It's who I've been most of my life. Sorry if that's not what you wanted to hear."

"I'm sorry, too." She sighed softly, the corner of her

mouth tugged down in a slight frown. "Good night, Wesley."

Bree climbed out of bed, gathered her towel and wrapped it around her again.

"Are you angry with me?" He sat up in bed, pulling the sheet up around his waist.

"No, of course not." There was pity and sadness in her voice. "I just think it's better if I sleep in my room. In case your mother comes looking for one of us in the morning."

Her excuse wasn't very convincing to either of them.

"I don't expect her to hobble up the steps. That was the whole point of moving her downstairs. If anything, she'll call upstairs." Wes kept his voice even. It needed to sound as if he was stating a fact, rather than the passionate plea it was.

He liked the idea of waking up to Bree in his arms.

Bree didn't acknowledge his statement. "See you at breakfast."

She exited through the bathroom door. He groaned when the distinct click of the door locking on the other side of the bathroom indicated she had no intention of returning.

Wes groaned, one arm folded behind his head. He should be glad Bree was honoring his request to keep their relationship casual. Instead, he was pouting like a child whose favorite toy had just been taken away.

Chapter 16

"Another trip with Wes, huh?" Bex's observation was more than a passing interest.

"Uh-huh." Bree turned away from Bex. They were using the video messaging app on her phone, which was propped on the nightstand. She stuffed her makeup bag into her luggage and zipped it. When she finally turned back to the phone, her friend had her arms crossed and one eye cocked. "What?"

"You know what. This isn't just business anymore, and it's obviously escalated beyond banging-buddy status. I'm worried about you. I don't want to see you get hurt." Bex's tone had shifted from exasperation to genuine concern.

"I won't." Her statement lacked conviction.

"Even you don't believe that."

It'd been more than a month since she and Wes had

taken their trip to Asheville. They'd continued their affair in secret, not even telling their best friends. But Bex knew her too well. She'd threatened to hop the next plane to Pleasure Cove if Bree didn't level with her.

So she'd told Bex the truth. She and Wes were friends who just happened to also enjoy sleeping together. A lot. But they were not a couple. Nor would they become one, because that wasn't what either of them wanted right now.

That part was a lie. One Bex saw right through. It was the reason she was so concerned.

Though she tried to allay her friend's concerns, they both knew the truth. In the recesses of her heart, Bree quietly believed Wes to be The Trifecta. The elusive man who would satisfy her body, heart and mind.

Each moment spent with Wesley Adams convinced her that he was the man with whom she could happily spend the rest of her life.

Though their no-strings agreement still stood, Bree was sure Wes cared for her more than he was willing to let on.

It was in his kiss. In his touch. In his voice when he whispered in her ear in the wee hours of the morning. It was in the depths of his dark eyes when he made love to her. In his stolen glances at her when he thought no one else was looking.

What they shared was more than sex or even friendship.

Bree wouldn't call it love, but it was deeper than lust or affection. Still, if Wes wasn't willing to explore his feelings for her, what did it matter? The end of summer would bring the volleyball tournament they'd both worked so hard on, and eventually, the end of their relationship. He'd stay in Pleasure Cove and she'd return to California, as if what they'd shared over the summer meant nothing.

The thought made her chest heavy with grief.

"I can handle whatever happens between us this time." Bree hoped her tone was more convincing.

"Then go to London and have a good time with your *friend*." An uneasy smile curled the edges of Bex's mouth. "How's his mom?"

"She's doing well." A wide smile tightened Bree's cheeks when she thought of Lena. Wes had hired an aide to help his mother around the house. Still, he'd visited Lena each week and Bree had accompanied him twice—at Lena's insistence. She went gladly, because she genuinely enjoyed Lena's company. "The air cast came off yesterday and she's getting around well. Still, I hate that neither of us will be here."

"You sound like a dutiful daughter-in-law." Bex peered into the camera, one eyebrow raised.

"She's an amazing woman. Funny and interesting. I can't help but adore her."

"Just don't get too attached. Walking away from Wes at the end of the summer means walking away from his mother, too."

The doorbell rang and Bree said goodbye to her friend, glad not to have to respond to Bex's very salient point.

It was too late. She'd already fallen for Wes and his mom.

A noise startled Wes awake. According to his mobile, it was a little after three in the morning. Yet,

Bree was no longer in bed. He followed the sound to his sitting room.

The lights were off, but he could make out Bree's form as she stood in front of the large windows that had enticed him into purchasing the flat. She stared into the distance at London's skyline.

"Is everything okay?"

"Everything is fine." She turned toward him, her face barely visible in the light streaming through the window. "Sorry, I didn't mean to wake you. I couldn't sleep. Figured it was a good time to take in this beautiful view."

"I fell for this place the moment I saw that view." He studied her silhouette in the moonlight. Wearing the sheer white lingerie he'd surprised her with, she managed to look naughty and angelic all at once.

"You look amazing." He stood behind her, slipped his arms around her waist and planted soft kisses on her warm neck. Inhaled her scent. Her soft murmur vibrated against his chest, making him want her more. Wes pressed his body to hers as he slipped the white fabric from her shoulder and trailed kisses there. "And as much as I love seeing you in this, what I'd really like is to see you out of it again."

Bree blushed in the moonlight, the corner of her mouth curling in an adorable grin that warmed him.

He couldn't resist smiling in response.

They'd been carrying on their affair for more than a month. Bree had initiated things that night in Asheville. Yet, at her core she was demure and, at times, bashful. He loved that she could be both a wily, determined temptress and the sweet, blushing girl next door.

"You have a big meeting this morning, remember?"

"It's this afternoon," he whispered in her ear, his lips brushing her skin. "Gives me plenty of time to spend with you."

"I like the sound of that." Bree turned around, her gaze meeting his as she slid one hand down his chest and beneath his waistband, taking him in her palm.

Wes sucked in a deep breath as she palmed his heated flesh. Her cool hand warmed as it glided up and down his shaft.

Her nostrils flared and the corner of her mouth curled with satisfaction. She seemed to enjoy the power she had over him as she stroked him, bringing him closer to the edge.

He cradled her face and claimed her mouth in a frantic kiss. Bree had him teetering on the edge. But he was desperate to be inside her again. To stare into those brown eyes, her bare, sweat-slickened skin pressed to his, as he erupted with pleasure.

Wes scooped her in his arms and she squealed, looping her arms around his neck so she wouldn't fall. He carried her to his bed, each of them shedding their clothing. He settled between her thighs and trailed kisses down her neck and between her breasts.

"You do realize I wasn't finished in there."

"But I nearly was, and we couldn't have that."

Scraping one beaded tip between his teeth, he gently teased it with his tongue. Bree squirmed beneath him. Her soft, sensual murmur stoked the fire building inside him.

Wes hated that he'd pulled the heavy curtains shut. He wanted the satisfaction of seeing Bree's lovely face as she called his name in the throes of her climax. A delight he never tired of.

He sheathed himself, then entered her slowly, groaning with pleasure as her snug heat welcomed him.

They moved together, heat building between them and a light sheen of sweat clinging to their skin. Bree's murmurs grew louder. Her breath came faster. She repositioned her legs and pressed her bare feet to his shoulders, allowing him to penetrate deeper.

She clutched the sheets, her back arched as she called his name, riding the wave of her orgasm. Nearly there, he continued his thrusts until his spine stiffened and he shuddered, cursing and moaning. Calling her name.

Breathless and sweaty, he gathered her in his arms and kissed her damp hair.

Bree Evans was the first woman who'd made him question the wisdom of his commitment to remaining unattached. She made him want to believe he was capable of giving her the things she wanted.

Love. Marriage. A family.

More and more, he'd allowed himself to imagine what it would be like to have those things with her. And it didn't feel stifling or confining. The images in his head filled him with warmth and contentment.

He could get used to having Bree in his bed every night, but he wouldn't delude himself by believing he could become something he wasn't. He'd already ruined one woman's life and caused them both irrevocable harm. He wouldn't do that to Bree. No matter how much he wanted her.

Chapter 17

"He's a pretty spectacular fellow, isn't he?"

The woman's voice startled Bree from what she often found herself doing these days—stealing loving glances at Wesley Adams when she thought no one was looking. His event manager, Nadia, obviously was.

The woman had done a poor job of hiding her disbelief when Wes had introduced her as a friend. Standing in the corner, staring at Wes like a lovelorn fool, didn't help.

"He is…very good at what he does, I mean," Bree clarified as she sipped her champagne. Wes and his team were working the party. So they weren't drinking. She had no such constraints. "I've learned a lot from him since we started working on the project together."

"I'll bet." Nadia was barely able to hold back her

grin. "He's taught me quite a lot about the event-planning and promotions business. Still, I've a lot to learn before I'll be anywhere near as gifted as he is."

"Well, he's certainly confident in you," Bree reassured the woman with a smile. "He'd never have entrusted his business to you if he wasn't."

"Thank you." Nadia beamed. "And if you don't mind me saying so, I've known him long enough to realize that what he feels for you is special." She looked over at Wes, who stood on the other side of the room staring at Bree. "I've never seen him light up the way he does when he looks at you. He's completely smitten and it scares him half to death."

A soft smile curved the edge of Bree's mouth and her cheeks warmed as she returned his affectionate gaze. Bree wanted to believe that what Nadia was saying was true. That Wes reciprocated her growing feelings for him.

The warmth she'd felt moments earlier gave way to a dull ache in her chest and a knot in her belly.

She returned her attention to Nadia. "It's not what you think."

"Maybe. Or maybe I'm right and you two are both wrong about what this is." Nadia squeezed her arm and disappeared into the crowd.

Bree released a long, slow breath, her heart beating quickly. They'd grown closer during their two weeks in London. Each day together had felt more intimate, but now their trip was coming to an end.

They'd fallen into an easy rhythm. Making love in the mornings and chatting over breakfast. Dinner together and nights that ended in the same manner they began. In each other's arms.

While Wes worked with his small team to hire more staff and finalize plans for a huge corporate party, Bree worked on the tournament and her own projects. She'd had video and phone conferences with Bex and the marketing consultant they'd hired to help them plan and promote their volleyball camps the following year.

Still, Wes had insisted on taking her to see all of the tourist attractions she hadn't been able to squeeze into her previous working trips to London. Visits to the Tower of London, Kensington Palace and Westminster Abbey. A turn on the London Eye—the giant Ferris wheel on the south bank of the River Thames. A romantic evening stroll across London Bridge and a view of the city from the hauntingly beautiful attached skyscraper—the Shard.

She'd been incredibly happy, and it seemed that Wes was, too. So why did he seem so terrified by the prospect of exploring the feelings they had for each other?

It was a question she'd revisited time and again. Yet, she hadn't wanted to broach the subject with him. She'd willingly agreed to a secret, no-strings-attached fling with Wes. Insisted that she was cosmopolitan enough to handle such an affair. So she'd grin and bear the pain that knotted her belly whenever she considered what would happen once the tournament had ended and they went their separate ways.

"Enjoying the party?" Wes stood beside her.

"Yes." Bree finished her glass of champagne and set it on the tray of a server walking by. "But I think I'll head back to your place. I feel like I'm a distraction to you. Besides, I need to call my mother and yours."

"You're a pleasant distraction. My favorite kind." He smiled warmly. "And as for my mom, I'm grateful you've been so patient with her, but if she's become a nuisance, I'll talk to her."

"Don't you dare. I enjoy spending time with her. I promise." She double-checked that the spare key Wes gave her was in her clutch, then snapped it shut. "See you back at the flat?"

"At least let me hail a taxi for you." Wes frowned.

"I'll be fine." Bree made her way to the exit, hoping that Nadia was right. And that Wes missed her as much as she was already missing him.

Despite all of the noise and movement swirling around him, Wes was focused on one thing—Brianna Evans walking away from him. A thought that had occupied a growing space in his brain.

He shouldn't worry about what would happen at the project's end. He should just enjoy every moment they had together. Stop worrying about the future and commiserating over his past. Live in the now.

Yet, losing her was all he could think of.

Though he couldn't rightly claim to be losing her when they'd be parting ways at his insistence.

"She's even nicer in person." Nadia had a way of sneaking up on him. "I see why you fancy her so."

Wes didn't respond to Nadia's attempt to gauge his relationship with Bree. It was safer to talk business instead.

"How are the two potential new hires doing?" His gaze swept the room, in search of any small details that might have fallen through the cracks.

"Smashing. It's too bad we can only afford to bring one of them onboard. Don't know how we'll choose."

"Maybe we won't have to." Wes held back a grin when Nadia's eyes widened. He'd been so preoccupied with business and Bree that he hadn't told her the news. "I've been talking with the Westbrooks over the past few weeks. They'd like to make us the official event-planning professionals for their London headquarters."

Nadia squeezed his arm and mimicked a silent squeal. "I thought you were determined to do this without them."

"I love and admire the Westbrooks, but I didn't want to feel beholden to them. I went against everyone's advice in starting this business—including Liam and his father. I needed to show them I could make it a success without their family's power and wealth behind me." He shrugged. "I've done that here."

"And in the US? I know your best mate begged you to help him out on short notice, but I get the sense there's more to it than that. Was working with Brianna the carrot that finally won you over?" Nadia grinned.

"Didn't realize she was involved when I agreed to it," he reminded her. An involuntary smile tightened his cheeks. "But working with her has turned out to be a highlight."

"I knew it. You're completely gaga over her, aren't you?" Nadia could barely contain her excitement.

"How is it you're more excited about this than my news about Westbrook International?" He raised a brow. "Especially since I'm promoting you to president of UK operations by the end of the year if everything works out in the US."

This time Nadia's squeal wasn't silent. With the ruckus going on around them, few people noticed. She hugged him.

"I can't believe it. Thank you for your faith in me. I was sure you'd bring some heavy hitter in to head things up here if the project went well across the pond."

"You've been with me since the beginning. Back when we were working out of that mangy old flat. You were there every day and worked solely on commission. How could you think I'd trust anyone else to head up the business here?"

"You're making me blush." Nadia swiped a finger beneath the corner of her eye and sniffled. "Don't expect this to put a stop to me meddling in your love life."

"I don't have a love life."

"Precisely. But you deserve to be happy with someone like Brianna. I quite like her. So don't you dare let her get away." Nadia elbowed him playfully, but then her voice turned somber. "If you care for her the way it seems you do, you'll never forgive yourself if you let her go."

Wes massaged the knot that had formed at the back of his neck.

If only it was that easy.

Chapter 18

Brianna stood at the window taking a mental picture of the view from Wesley's flat. She was trying to memorize it and everything about their past two weeks together in London.

The soft strains of Duke Ellington and John Coltrane's version of "In a Sentimental Mood" drifted from the multi-room audio wired throughout his flat. She'd been listening to the song on repeat. It was Wesley's favorite classic jazz standard. She'd heard it often in the weeks they'd been together, each time with more appreciation than the time before.

On their final night in London together, the song captured her mood brilliantly. Ellington's ethereal piano notes combined with Coltrane's smooth, somber sax made for a brooding, introspective piece reflective of both joy and sadness.

Exactly what she was feeling now.

Her chest filled with warmth as she reflected on the two weeks they'd spent together in London. Yet, a pervasive sense of sadness made her heart ache.

They'd never be in London together again. The city that had originally brought them together.

She inhaled the unbuttoned blue oxford shirt she wore over her bra and panties. The same shirt he'd been wearing before they'd stripped each other naked and made love.

"I'm officially packed and ready for our early morning departure. I'm surprised you're not asleep." Wes joined her at the window.

"Committing this remarkable view to memory." Bree fiddled with the collar of the shirt, hoping Wesley hadn't caught her sniffing its scent moments earlier. They'd shared so many special moments in London. Moments in which they'd grown closer.

London was now inextricably linked with Wesley Adams.

"It isn't as if you'll never return. To London, I mean." His gaze drifted from hers. They were silent for a moment before he shifted the topic. "I've obviously convinced you of the many virtues of 'In a Sentimental Mood.'"

"It's brilliant. Evocative of so many powerful emotions."

"Come here." Wes moved toward the center of the room and extended his hand. When Bree joined him, he took her hand in his and looped an arm around her waist. "Dance with me."

His soft, intimate plea filled her body with heat. A charge of electricity ran along her skin.

She swayed with Wes, her ear pressed to his chest, listening to the thud of his heart as it beat against his strong chest. Her eyes drifted closed for a moment as they swayed and turned about the room ever so slightly with each step.

His chin propped on her head, Wes cradled her closer, neither of them speaking.

The connection they shared was more than sex. More than friendship.

So why was Wes so determined to walk away from the very thing they both seemed to want and need? What was Wes really afraid of?

Bree wanted to ask, but the words wouldn't come. To quiet the pervasive questions that danced in her head, she shifted attention back to the song.

"You said Miles Davis and Thelonious Monk are your favorite jazz artists. So why is a collaboration between Ellington and Coltrane your favorite jazz song?"

"Aside from the brilliance of the collaboration and the complexity of the piece?" Wes's voice rumbled against her ear. "Got my own sentimental connection to the song." He paused so long it seemed he'd decided against divulging it. "My favorite memory of my parents is them dancing to this song."

"That's beautiful." Something about his admission made tears instantly well in her eyes. Bree wasn't sure if she was moved by the poignancy of the story, or by his willingness to share it with her.

"Your mom showed me some old family pictures." Bree hadn't mentioned it before because Wes wasn't inclined to reminisce about his dad. But tonight, he seemed open to it. "Lena is gorgeous now, but she looked like a glamorous movie star in all her photos. And you guys all look so happy."

"In the beginning, my mom was, and I think my dad wanted to be. But his passion was music, being on the road traveling. Maybe he really did love us. But he loved music and life on the road more."

"Wes, I'm sorry." She squeezed him tightly. Bree understood the pain and rejection Wes felt. It was a pain that could only truly be understood by someone who'd endured it, too.

"Don't be." Wes slid his hands beneath the shirt she wore. His rough hands glided along her warm skin. He traced a scar from an old surgery with his thumb.

Bree tensed, self-conscious about the ugly scar. She'd had it incorporated into the tattoo on her side to camouflage the imperfection.

"Does it hurt?" His soft, warm gaze met hers.

"No, and neither does this one." She slipped the shirt from her shoulder enough to reveal a scar that remained from her shoulder surgery a few years ago. "But they've ruined my bikini game." She tried to keep her breathing even as she maintained his heated gaze.

"I assure you that nothing could possibly mar the sight of you in a bikini. Besides, with a one-piece like the one you wore in my hot tub that day…who needs one?" He gripped her bare waist and pulled her closer to him again as he leaned in and whispered in her ear. "By the way, that swimsuit…you weren't playing fair. A man with less willpower would've caved."

"Your concept for the tournament was best, so it's good you were strong enough to resist my charms." She glided a hand up his bare chest. "But I won when it really counted."

"I assume you're talking about when I gave in on other aspects of the tournament—like the stage layout and the celebrities we invited." His sexy mouth curved in a knowing grin that did wicked things to her. Made her want to do wicked things to him.

"Then, too." Bree's cheeks tightened as she tried to hold back a smirk.

Wes kissed her, tightening his grip on her waist as one hand drifted down to squeeze her bottom, pulling her hard against the ridge beneath the fly of his jeans.

She parted her lips and he slipped his warm tongue inside her mouth. Her heart beat faster and her temperature rose as he kissed her hard and deep, with a passion that made her dizzy with want.

Wes turned her around and slipped the shirt from her shoulders. He loosened her bra and let it drift to the floor. When he teased her hardened nipples, her spine stiffened and she sucked in a breath.

He turned her head, capturing her mouth in a bruising kiss that made her core pulse. Wes trailed a hand down her belly, slipping it inside her panties, damp with her desire for him. He teased the bundle of nerves as she moved against his hand. Her heart beat faster as pleasure built in her core. When he pulled his hand away, she released an involuntary whimper, desperate for release.

His eyes met hers, his chest heaving. What she saw there made her weak with want. Wes's gaze radiated heat, passion and raw emotion.

His gaze mirrored everything she'd been feeling. An emotion she hadn't wanted to name. One that felt a lot like love. And looked like what she saw reflected in Wesley's eyes.

Wes took her to his bed and made love to her. It was intensely passionate, but also deeply emotional, in a way it hadn't been before. Things had shifted between them.

Body trembling and her climax building as he held her gaze, something suddenly became very clear.

She wanted to be his. Now and always.

He seemed to want it, to ache for it, too.

Bree blurted out the thing that was on her heart. The one thing she hadn't wanted to say aloud.

"Wes, I love you."

Wes, still recovering from his own release, seemed stunned by Bree's admission.

She'd read him wrong. Had seen what she so desperately wanted to see.

Wes lay beside her, awkward silence stretching between them, making the seconds feel like minutes. Finally, he turned on his side, his head propped on his fist. "Bree, I—I…"

"It's okay." Bree sat up abruptly, her words accompanied by a nervous laugh that only seemed to make him pity her. She dragged her fingers through her hair. "I shouldn't have said that. I was just…you know." She swiped a finger beneath her eye. "Let's talk about something else while I pretend not to be embarrassed that I just said that."

"You have nothing to be embarrassed about, Bree." He stroked her arm. "It isn't you, I swear. I just can't—"

"Please…don't." She inhaled deeply, then forced a painful smile as tears sprung from her eyes. She quickly wiped them away. "Let's talk about something else. Anything. Please."

"Okay." He sat up, too. "Can I get you a glass of wine or something?"

"Wine would be great. Thank you."

While he moved about the kitchen, Bree turned on the bedside lamp, retrieved her underwear and slipped on a T-shirt and a pair of his boxers, since her pajamas were already packed in her luggage. She sat in one of the chairs near the window in his bedroom.

"The French Bordeaux Sauternes we bought at Borough Market." He handed her a glass.

Her hand trembled slightly as she accepted the glass. She took a long sip. Concentrated on the balance of sweetness and acidity. The flavor notes of apricot and honey. *Anything* but the fact that she'd just admitted to Wes that she loved him.

Wes joined her in the sitting area by the window, the space where he often sat and read in the mornings before he would start his day.

He swallowed hard. The words he wanted to say lodged painfully in his throat.

I love you, too.

He had no business saying them. Wouldn't give her false hope.

"You wanted to talk about something else." He set his glass on the small, shabby chic table between them. A salvaged piece he'd held onto from his college days because it was the first piece of furniture his mother had ever refinished. "So tell me, what's next in your career?"

Bree narrowed her gaze at him. It was another loaded topic. He'd known that before he asked her.

She'd been playing volleyball professionally for

well over a decade. With each passing year and each new injury, speculation about the end of her career swirled. Something it seemed Bex was experiencing as she fought to come back from her latest injury.

Still, he really wanted to know. Since they both seemed prone to deep introspection and spontaneous confession tonight, it seemed the perfect time to inquire.

"I hope to play a few more years. So now's the time for me to begin the transition from professional volleyball player to whatever comes next."

"And what is that?" Wes wasn't satisfied with her non-answer. "Will the volleyball camps be your full-time pursuit once you've retired?"

"That's what Bex wants."

"But what does Brianna want?" His voice softened.

"I'm not sure." She shrugged. "Volleyball has been my entire life since I was in middle school. I've sacrificed so much to be the best at what I do. I'm not completely sure where I go from there. Professionally speaking."

They were both silent for a moment, then he asked, "In your heart of hearts, what is it you'd like to be doing, more than anything, outside of playing volleyball?"

"I don't know…"

"I think you do." He swapped his untouched wineglass with her empty one, then sat back in his chair and surveyed her. "Maybe you're reluctant to share it with me, but—"

"What I'm doing now," she said quickly, picking up her wineglass and taking a sip. "Not *this*, obviously." She held up the wineglass and they both laughed.

A little of the tension between them eased. "I mean being a spokesperson for important causes. Helping people. Making a difference." A genuine smile lifted her cheeks and lit her eyes. "Going to visit with sick children at hospitals. Talking to high-risk children at inner-city schools and at boys' and girls' clubs. Helping them see that they matter. That no matter how big their dreams are, they're attainable. They just need to believe in themselves and be willing to work for it. But a good support system helps. And I'd like to be that for those kids."

Bree caught Wes staring at her and her cheeks flushed. She took another sip of her wine as she gazed out of the window. "I sound like a corny do-gooder, right?"

"Look at me, Bree." He shifted forward in his seat as her gaze met his. "Never apologize for who you are. Every character trait, every physical scar…they all make you the remarkable warrior goddess you are. So don't apologize for any of it. Got it?"

She was silent for a moment, then nodded.

"Good." He smiled and her shoulders relaxed. "If that's what you really want to do, do it. Kids like us, who came from nothing, they desperately need someone to believe in them. To support their dreams and give them opportunities they wouldn't have had otherwise."

Bree took another sip of her wine. "The trouble is, if I don't keep playing, in some capacity, I'm no longer relevant, and I won't get opportunities like this."

"Make your own. Start your own organization."

"It's not that simple."

"Isn't it? It's not like you'd have to do everything

yourself. A charity is like any other business. Hire the best people to run it for you."

Bree seemed unconvinced.

"Seems you've given this some thought, but something about the idea scares you. What is it?"

"It seems overwhelming, to say the least. Besides, it's such an important task. I can't let them down. What if I fail?"

"What if you succeed? Think of how many lives you could change?"

"Have you always been this confident?" She crooked an eyebrow as she studied him.

For a moment, he was sure she could see right through him to the scared little boy wearing hand-me-downs at a boarding school filled with children of the rich and famous. "I had to learn. Survival of the fittest, you know?"

She nodded. "I was one of only a handful of minority kids at my entire private school. The only one there on scholarship. So, I worked hard to prove that I was this perfect little girl. That I belonged there as much as anyone else. Still, there's always this part of me that wonders deep down if I'm really good enough." Bree stood quickly and swiped dampness from the corner of her eyes. "It's late. I need to get ready for bed."

Wes sighed as she disappeared behind the bathroom door. If only he could tell Bree the truth. It was him who wasn't good enough for her.

Wes lay awake, more than an hour after they'd gone to bed, watching Bree as she slept. He cared for her more than any woman he'd ever known. And he wanted to believe he deserved her. That they could be happy together forever.

He turned onto his back and stared at the ceiling, trying to quiet the voice that implored him to trust her with the truth.

That he wanted her, and only her.

He had his rules. Rules designed to keep him from ever needlessly hurting anyone again. He was determined not to break those rules by falling for her.

And yet…he already had.

He'd tried to pretend that what they shared was a symbiotic fusion of sex and friendship. One they could both easily walk away from.

But Bree had changed the game.

She'd shown him how gratifying it was to forge a deep connection with someone who knew him in ways no one else did.

But if he truly cared for her, he'd stick to the plan.

He wouldn't take a chance on disappointing her the way his father had disappointed his mother. Or the way he'd once disappointed someone who'd loved him more than he deserved.

Wes glanced at Bree again. They'd had an incredible time in London. It would be hard to return to this flat without thinking of her in his home, in his bed and in his life. And how happy it made him.

But he'd been playing a dangerous game with Bree's heart. Fooling himself into thinking they could do this without either of them getting hurt.

He did love Bree. And because he loved her, he would let her go.

He'd never hurt anyone that way again. The price was far too steep.

Chapter 19

Brianna had broken the rules of their little game, and now Wes was making her pay.

They'd both downplayed her misstep the previous night. However, the next morning, he was polite, but withdrawn. At the very least, distracted. Though they'd both slept during much of it, their nonstop flight home had been uncharacteristically quiet.

Bree silently cursed herself again for saying those three little words their final night in London. It was the perfect way to ruin a sublime trip and kill the mood with her no-strings-attached lover.

Wes put the last of her luggage upstairs and returned to the living room, where she sifted through a stack of mail and a few postcards. He shoved his hands into his pockets, his gaze not quite meeting hers.

"Look, I know you must be tired. Why don't I stay at my place tonight?"

A stab in the heart would've been less painful.

"Of course. I'll see you… I'll guess you'll let me know when."

She put down the mail and went to the kitchen. Bree opened the fridge, pulled over the trash can and tossed spoiled and expired food into it.

"Bree, I don't want to hurt you. You know that. But maybe this was a mistake." Wes made his way to the kitchen.

"I know we agreed not to let things get serious, and I'm the one at fault here. I made the mistake of thinking you had, you know…feelings. Like a regular human." Bree poured the remainder of a half gallon of milk down the drain, rinsed the bottle and tossed it in the recycle bin.

"You think I'm saying this because I *don't* have feelings? You couldn't be more wrong."

"Then level with me. What's this really about?"

"I am leveling with you, but you won't believe me."

Bree closed the fridge. She struggled to be calm and mature about this. After all, what was the difference between her and her stalkerish ex if she couldn't accept that it was over?

"If you've tired of me and you're ready to move on…fine. And maybe I'm wrong, but I don't think that's it. You act as if you don't want intimacy or a real relationship, but I know that isn't true. I see the truth in your eyes whenever we're together. What I can't figure out is what you're so afraid of?"

He narrowed his gaze, as if she'd struck a nerve, but he didn't respond.

"Talk to me, Wes. Whatever it is, just say it." She stepped closer to him, stopping short of touching him. "Is there someone else?"

"Bree, there's no one in the world I'd rather be with. But I'm not prepared to make the kind of promises you're looking for."

"What the hell does that even mean?" Bree stood tall, her arms folded, despite wanting to dissolve into tears. She refused to give him the satisfaction of knowing how deeply his rejection cut.

"I'm trying to be completely honest with you, Bree. I won't be like my old man, making promises he couldn't keep. I won't do that to you. To us. I need to be sure."

"Of what? That no one better will come along?" She glared at him. "And what am I supposed to do? Warm your bed, fingers crossed, hoping one day you'll be ready? No thank you."

"It's not like that. Believe me."

"I don't. And I don't believe this is just about your dad walking out on you. People get divorced. Parents leave. And yeah, we both got saddled with a shitty parent. But we don't have to be them. I'm certainly not going to just lie down and die because I'm afraid I'll be like mine."

Wesley's eyes widened, his mouth falling open. She'd stunned him with a strike to the jugular.

Maybe it wasn't fair for her to bring up his dad, but Wes had opened the door to it when he'd used his old man as an excuse.

Bree sighed, no longer able to take the silence between them.

"I think maybe you're right. This was a mistake. I

take full responsibility. You were very clear from the beginning. I should've taken your word for it instead of pushing you."

"I'm not saying we can't be friends."

"Nor am I." Bree held her head high. "But right now, let's just focus on putting on a kick-ass tournament. Okay?"

Wes's eyes reflected every bit of the pain it caused her to utter those words. He didn't move or speak.

"So that's it?" Wes cleared his throat, his hands shoved in his pockets.

"I think it has to be. But we'll always have London, right?" She forced a smile, not allowing the tears that stung her eyes to fall.

"Always." He cradled her face and kissed her goodbye.

She waited for the click of the door closing behind Wes before she crumbled onto the sofa, tears streaming down her face.

She'd gambled and lost.

Maybe she'd played her hand too soon. Or perhaps the real mistake had been that she'd dared to play the game at all.

Wes straightened his collar and closed his eyes briefly as he exhaled a long, slow breath. It was exactly two weeks before his best friend's wedding and nearly three weeks since he and Bree had ended their affair.

He'd been in Las Vegas for two days with Liam and around twenty of their friends. But it hadn't been enough to lift the testy mood he'd been in since last he'd seen Bree. She'd returned to California the day after they'd ended things, and she'd attended the last two meetings about the volleyball tournament via video conference.

Yet, she'd kept her promise. She'd kept things civil and pleasant between them. As if nothing at all had happened. He'd called her directly a week prior to get her opinion on a change to the celebrity-chef lineup. Brianna answered the phone and had been as syrupy sweet as the sweet tea his mother made. With the issue resolved, he'd tried to make small talk, but she'd politely excused herself to take another call.

She'd saved him from himself. Had he spoken to her at any length, he'd have confessed to missing her every single day.

It was best that Bree was there in California and he was in Vegas celebrating his best friend's impending nuptials.

Wes had expended a tremendous amount of effort the past two days trying to be a proper best man. Immersing himself in the celebratory spirit. But he'd spent most of the weekend attempting to mask the cavernous hole Bree's absence left in his heart.

Wes knocked on the door of Liam's hotel suite. His friend answered the door in the midst of a video chat with his fiancée's daughters, the two little girls he adored as if they were his own.

"Say hello to Uncle Wes." Liam turned the phone toward him.

Sofia and Gabriella waved at him. "Hi, Uncle Wes!"

His mouth curled in an involuntary smile. His first genuine smile of the day. Since he'd been living in Pleasure Cove he'd gotten to know the girls and he now understood why Liam adored them.

He chatted with Sofie and Ella briefly before Liam finished his conversation and promised the girls he'd see them soon.

"Go ahead and say it, mate. They've got me wrapped around their little fingers." Liam grinned.

"That's like saying the earth is round. It's already an established fact." Wes sat on the huge sectional sofa, avoiding the cushion that reeked of beer. Liam's brother, Hunter, had spilled some on it the night before. "Besides, I'm happy for you. You know that."

"I do." Liam poured each of them two fingers of Scotch, then handed him one. He sat in a nearby chair. "I also know you thought I'd gone off my trolley for giving up my confirmed bachelorhood to become an instant dad."

"Also an established fact." Wes chuckled softly, taking a sip of the premium Scotch—Liam's preferred drink. "But I'm man enough to admit when I'm wrong."

"I should expect an apology, should I?" Liam raised an eyebrow incredulously. "Well, for goodness sake, man, get on with it."

"I honestly believed you'd be sacrificing your way of life and your independence when you took on Maya and her daughters. I was wrong. You weren't giving up your life, you were gaining a fuller, richer life. One that's made you happier than I've ever known you to be."

"That's saying a lot since we've known each other since we were thirteen." Liam grinned. "I used to hear chaps say that some woman or other was the best thing that ever happened to them, and I'd think to myself they must have lived sad and dreary lives before marriage. But now I understand, because Maya and the girls are truly the best thing to ever happen to me."

"No cold feet, then? Not even a little?"

"Not even the tiniest little bit." A broad smile lit Liam's eyes. "We already have such a wonderful life together. I look forward to making it official."

"I envy you, my friend."

"I'd much prefer you find your own." Liam tilted his head as he assessed him. "Tell me this foul mood you've been in for the past few weeks has nothing to do with Bree returning to California."

"Why would it?" Not a lie, simply a question.

"You tell me." Liam wore a supremely smug expression.

"I know it's your stag party weekend, but that doesn't mean you get a pass on being a nosy, obnoxious bastard." Wes finished his Scotch and set the glass on the table.

"No? Why should it be different from any other day?"

"Don't tempt me to launch a lamp or something at that big head of yours." Wes picked up a pillow and flung it at his friend and he tossed it back.

The lock clicked and Hunter stepped into the room along with Liam's two brothers-in-law to-be, Nate Johnston and Dash Williams.

"Don't remember seeing a pillow fight on the agenda for the weekend." Hunter put two cases of bitter on the bar and plopped down on the sofa. "Are you two going to braid each other's hair next?"

Wes and Liam picked up pillows and tossed them at Hunter simultaneously.

"Guess that makes us the only two grown-ups in

the room," Nate said to Dash, as he put a case of imported beer on the bar and sat on a bar stool.

"Then we've definitely moved up in the world. The girls will be glad to hear it." Dash chuckled.

Wes checked his watch and stood. "The party limo will be here in ten. Where is Maya's brother Cole?"

Liam scrolled through the messages on his phone. "Cole will meet us at the limo."

"Then we'd better head downstairs. Everyone else is meeting us at the limo, too."

They loaded the beer onto a luggage cart and headed out into the hallway. Dash pushed the cart onto the partially full elevator. Nate and Hunter got on, too. Wes was about to join them when Liam grabbed his arm.

"You go on. We'll catch the next lift." Liam turned to him as the elevator doors closed.

"Look, I know we were joking around in there, but Bree really is phenomenal. If you're this miserable because she's gone, that should tell you something, mate."

"I like her, okay?" Wes looked away from his friend. "I maybe even love her. But what if I'm wrong? What if in six months or two years I feel differently?"

"Love is a gamble, my friend. None of us knows what will happen tomorrow or next year. But if you truly care for her, tell her how you feel and why."

"What if I tell her the truth and she hates me for it?"

"Then you'll know she's not the one for you."

Wesley's chest felt hollow at the thought of peering into his favorite brown eyes and seeing genuine contempt.

Still, in light of the pain her absence had caused him, it was worth the risk.

Chapter 20

Bree stood on her back deck watering her poor, neglected flowers and enjoying the California sun. She put down the watering can and sat at the patio table with Bex, who was reviewing samples for the camp logo.

"Another cup of coffee?" Bree offered.

"No thanks." Bex studied her for a moment, then sighed. "Look, I'm just going to say this. I was wrong about you and Wesley."

"No, you weren't. You were exactly right. You said I would get hurt and I did. I should've listened."

"But you were so happy. You practically glowed on video chat." Bex closed her laptop. "It was annoying."

"Then you should be happy I'm…" Bree sighed, not wanting to finish the sentence.

"Miserable?" Bex squeezed her arm. "I could never be happy about that."

Bree checked her phone. No calls or text messages from Wes.

"He hasn't contacted me, so obviously he doesn't feel the same."

"Maybe that's because you cut him off so abruptly last time he called." Bex had been there when she'd taken the call.

"It doesn't matter. He doesn't want a relationship, and I do. So there's really nothing for us to talk about."

"Start there. Wes doesn't seem like the typical guy who just can't be bothered to keep it in his pants. Something's got this guy spooked about being in a relationship. You need to find out what it is."

"I can't make him tell me."

"Then ask his mother. She adores you."

"I won't pry into his life behind his back. When he's ready to tell me, he will."

Bex pulled up a photo Bree had sent her. It was her and Wesley at the top of the Shard. She scrolled to another of them atop Looking Glass Rock.

"See what I mean? You never looked that happy when you were with that jerk Alex. Not even in the beginning. Can you believe he had the audacity to email me about you?"

Bree dropped her gaze, sinking her teeth into her lower lip.

"What aren't you telling me, Bree? Has Alex been bothering you?"

"He's left messages. I haven't answered any of them, but he keeps calling. And while I was in London, he sent a postcard to me in Pleasure Cove."

"He's stalking you?" Bex's nostrils flared. Her forehead and cheeks reddened.

"I wouldn't call it that. He's just having a really tough time taking no for an answer. Something I can relate to."

"You were *not* a stalker. A determined seductress? Yes. A stalker? Definitely not."

Bex picked up Bree's phone and handed it to her.

"You want me to call him?"

"No, I want you to call the police."

"Let's just take a minute and breathe, Bex. Alex will eventually get the message or he'll find someone new to harass."

"So you admit he's harassing you?"

"Yes… I mean, no. Look, I don't want to end up on some tacky gossip show, and that's exactly what's going to happen if I make that call." Bree tried to reason with her friend. Bex knew from experience how persistent the paparazzi could be.

"I don't know, Bree. Alex sounds a little unhinged right now. What if his behavior escalates?" Bex folded her arms, her eyebrows drawn together.

"If things get worse, I swear you'll be the first to know."

"What time does your flight leave tomorrow?"

"Ten."

"You should, at least, tell Wes about this guy." Bex frowned.

"It isn't his problem. It's mine. It'll be okay. I promise. Now, let's see those logo samples."

Bree opened Bex's laptop and studied the artwork proofs as if they were the only worry she had in the world.

* * *

Wes stepped outside his door as Bree descended her front stairs.

"Good morning, Wesley." She offered a polite wave.

Her willingness to speak first was a good sign, despite the formal address and schoolteacher tone.

"Hi." He caught up with her and fell in step as she walked toward the main building, where the meeting was being held. "Wasn't sure you'd be here in person for today's meeting."

"It's the last one before Liam goes on his honeymoon. So I thought I should be here."

"I'm glad you're here, Bree. I've missed you."

Bree didn't break her stride or in any way acknowledge his words.

Maybe Bree had found someone else. Someone who wasn't afraid to commit. Someone with less egregious sins in his past.

"I'm sorry about before. I was an ass—"

"On that we can agree." Bree gave him a quick glance.

"But not for the reasons you might think," Wes said quickly. "It's just that when you said…well, what you said, I panicked. Relationships aren't my usual MO. I wasn't sure how to respond."

She stopped and turned to him. "You seemed sure about it being a mistake for us to have gotten involved."

When Wes lowered his gaze, Bree walked away.

"Bree, I'm trying to explain how I felt…how I feel."

She stopped again and glared up at him. "I'll admit, maybe I said it too soon. But the fact that you seem incapable of saying the words doesn't bode well for us."

Bree checked the time on her phone.

"Look, if you want to talk about what went wrong with us...fine. But let's do it after the meeting. I need to have a clear head right now and this isn't helping."

"I'll throw some steaks on the grill, and we can talk over dinner." That would give him time to get his thoughts together. He couldn't afford a repeat performance of his blabbering-idiot show.

She shrugged her agreement.

It wasn't an enthusiastic acceptance, but at least she hadn't turned him down.

Chapter 21

Bree kicked off her heels and unzipped her skirt. It'd been a long, but productive meeting. They'd sold out of the majority of their sponsorships and were at nearly three quarters of their registration capacity.

They'd gotten the local shop owners onboard by opening the vendor opportunities up to them first at a special rate. Everything was organized and running smoothly and many of the local townsfolk had signed up to serve as volunteers for the event. They were in excellent shape.

Bree changed into shorts and a tank, then grabbed her phone to respond to a few emails before dinner. She opened the patio door and let the cool breeze drift in. The smell of charcoal indicated that Wes had already fired up the grill.

She opened the front door to get a nice cross breeze in the guest house.

"Hello, Brianna."

Bree froze, a chill running down her spine. Her hands trembled and her heart raced. She didn't need to look in those icy blue eyes to know whose voice it was.

"Alex, what are you doing here?"

His toothy smile quickly dissolved into an equally disturbing frown. "I've been trying to reach you for months. You haven't responded to any of my messages."

She stood taller, narrowing her gaze. "Then you should've taken the hint."

The frown morphed into a scowl. "I understand why you're treating me this way, Bree. But I just want to talk."

"There is *nothing* for us to talk about. Not now. Not ever." She stuffed her hands in her pockets, hoping he couldn't see how badly they were shaking.

"I've come all this way to talk to you. The least you could do is let me take you out to dinner, so I can explain. I know I wasn't the best person back then, but I'm different now. I just want to show you that I'm not that man anymore."

"Maybe you are different now. If so, that's great. But you put your hands on me, Alex. I can never trust you again."

"It was one time, and I told you how sorry I was. That I didn't mean to do it. I was so stressed out back then, you know?"

"That's not an acceptable excuse for how you treated me. I should've left you long before I did."

"I told you, I'm not that guy anymore." A vein bulged in his forehead. "If you can't go to dinner, we can talk now. I only need ten minutes. Let me come in. We can sit down and hash this out."

"I don't want to hash things out. I don't miss you or us or the way things were. I don't want any of it, and I don't want you. Please, just go away." She scanned the room for something she could use as a weapon if he tried to force his way inside the door. "I don't want to get the police involved, but I will if I have to."

Bree recognized the signs of rage building. The muscles of his neck corded, his pale skin was mottled and his nostrils flared.

"I'm simply asking for a chance to explain myself, and you're threatening to call the cops on me?" he practically shouted as he dragged his fingernails through his dirty blond hair.

Bree didn't flinch, determined not to show any fear. It was fear that fed the monster.

"I'd do it in an instant and happily watch them drag your ass to jail. That probably wouldn't go over too well with that investment bank of yours."

"You wouldn't."

"Try me." She stood her ground. Her chest heaved and her breath came in noisy pants as her own anger overtook any fear she might have had facing him again.

"Everything all right, babe?" Wes was suddenly behind her. He wrapped his arms around her waist possessively.

"Peachy." She wasn't sure when Wes had entered through her patio door, but she was grateful he was there.

"Who is this?" Alex's gaze shifted from Bree to Wes and back again.

"The man who plans to marry her. And the owner of an aluminum bat with your name on it if you don't turn around right now and walk your happy ass outta here. While you still can." Wes's voice was calm and his tone icy as he dropped his hand from her waist and stepped in front of her.

Alex huffed, his jaw clenched. "You're as crazy as she is. Who needs this? You two deserve each other."

He turned and stomped down the stairs to his Mercedes-Benz parked outside. Neither of them moved until he drove away.

When Alex's car left the lot, Bree released a noisy breath, her hands to her mouth.

"Are you okay, baby?" He gripped her shoulders gently. When she nodded, he pulled her into his arms and held her. Wes closed and locked the front door. "Here, come sit down."

He got her a bottle of water and sat on the sofa beside her.

She took a sip, her hands still shaking. "I can't believe he showed up here."

"Tell me everything you know about this guy."

"The short answer? Biggest mistake of my life. That's what happens when you don't listen to your gut," she added under her breath.

"Go on." He leaned forward intently.

Bree brought Wes up to speed on her history with Alex Hunt, and his persistent attempts to contact her over the past few months.

She drank more of her water. "That line about the bat...that was good. Sounds like something your mother would say."

"Who do you think gave me the bat?" Wes walked

over to the window and looked out of it again. "I don't trust this guy to act in his own best interest. You're staying with me tonight."

"Wes, I appreciate what you did. I really do. But I'm fine. Alex won't be back."

"Didn't seem like he was too good at taking a hint or following instructions." Wes crossed his arms, his expression grave. "Guys like that are unpredictable. You never know how far they'll take things. Do you have a restraining order against this guy?"

She shook her head. "No."

"Then get one."

"I don't want the negative publicity, especially with the tournament coming up. Nor do I want to be seen as a victim." She paced the floor. "That would tank my endorsement stock ten times faster than a male athlete being convicted of an actual crime."

"You don't want to be seen as a victim. I get that, but I'm far more concerned about you actually becoming one." A deep frown made his brows appear as angry slashes. "This isn't something to play with."

"And it isn't fair. I never asked for this."

Wes cupped her cheek and spoke softly, his eyes filled with concern. "I know it isn't, honey. But the priority is to keep you safe. You believe that taking action against this guy will make you look weak, but it will empower you. You, in turn, can empower other women dealing with the same bullshit. You want to help people? This is a way to do it."

"Okay." Bree nodded begrudgingly. "I promised Bex I'd get the police involved if the situation escalated."

"You should've told me about this guy earlier. We could've put a halt to this before it got this far."

"I know that we're friends, and you want to help, but I'm not looking for a man to save me. And I don't need a knight in shining armor who walks away the first time he gets freaked out or things get tough."

"Fair enough." Wes wiped his palms on his black basketball shorts. "Now, about why I have trouble saying…" He sighed, then stood again. "It'll be easier if I show you."

Wes led Bree through the patio door and over to his place. He went to his bedroom and retrieved the most precious thing he owned. A black leather photo album with gold lettering on front.

His heart hammered in his chest as he handed the photo album to Bree.

What would she think of him once she knew the truth?

He didn't doubt her discretion. But would she look at him differently? See him as the monster he saw in the mirror?

Bree seemed as nervous as he was. She opened the book reverently. As if it was an artifact that needed to be handled with care.

She studied the pictures on the first two pages. Pictures of the same little boy at various ages from newborn to about twelve years old.

"He's your son." She nearly whispered the words, her fingers delicately tracing the boy's nose and mouth. Mirror images of his own.

"Yes." Wes nodded, taking the seat across from her. "His name is Gray Grammerson."

Her eyes lit with recognition. "The facing capital

*G*s that form the door of the cage on your tattoo. That's for your son."

Wes didn't answer. He didn't need to.

She turned more pages. "Most of these photos were taken from a distance. So you obviously don't share custody of him."

"Right again."

"So he lives with his mother?" Bree stopped turning the pages.

"Not his bio mom. She gave him up for adoption without ever telling me. In fact, I'd never have known about my son had it not been for a mutual friend from university."

"That's awful. Why would she do that?"

"Probably because she didn't think I was worthy of being a father to our child. We weren't together by the time she learned about the pregnancy. I think she also wanted to punish me for hurting her."

Bree raised an eyebrow. "What did you do to make her hate you?"

"I was young and selfish. My life was about meaningless hookups. I wanted her, and she didn't want to be with someone who didn't love her. So I told her I did." He swallowed hard. "We were together a few weeks. Maybe a month. When I was ready to move on, she was devastated."

Bree's eyes were misty. Her expression relayed both disappointment and compassion. "What happened to her?"

"She was an American expat, too. She returned to America. At the time, I was a selfish little prick. I thought, good riddance. I had no idea…" He winced, his eyes not meeting hers. "I had no idea she was pregnant with my son. A few years later, a fellow class-mate contacted me. She'd run in to my ex, who told her about the baby. Our baby. She'd given him up without notifying me. I was devastated."

"Where's his mother now?"

"She's an international-aid worker stationed at one of the largest refugee camps in Uganda."

"Have you talked to her since you learned about your son?"

Wes's jaw clenched involuntarily at the thought of confronting Janine. He shook his head. "It's a conver-sation I can't imagine going well."

Bree studied a photo of Gray being pushed on a swing by his adoptive mother. "How'd you find him?"

"It's one of the few times I readily accepted help from the Westbrooks. Liam helped me find a detec-tive, who tracked down my son. When I found him, he was in a loving, wonderful family with good parents. I didn't have the heart to disrupt their lives."

"So how'd you get the pictures? The detective?"

"He dug up everything he could find at the out-set. A lot of the pictures were on his adoptive par-ents' social-media pages. I have him do a checkup twice a year, just to make sure everything is okay with my son."

"He's so handsome. Just like his father." Bree smiled faintly as she thumbed through the book, and Wes felt as if she'd given him a lifeline.

She hadn't condemned him or walked out in dis-gust at the pig he'd been back then. When she reached the end of the book she closed it carefully and set it on the coffee table. She stood in front of him, opened her arms and embraced him.

He hugged her tightly, overwhelmed with a sense of relief and gratitude.

"I'm so sorry." She kissed his head. "It makes sense now, how you feel. But, honey, you can't punish yourself for the rest of your life. What you did was wrong, but you're *not* the one who gave your son away. And look at the effort you put into finding him and into making sure he's safe."

Wes didn't speak. Pain, shame and regret swirled inside him, along with a deep affection for her. Bree's warmth and compassion soothed his soul.

Made him feel human again.

"You aren't the person you were then, Wes. Let go of the guilt and forgive yourself. I know your son wouldn't want you to torture yourself this way."

"What makes you believe that?"

"Because I'd give anything for my bio mother to love me even half as much as you love your son." Her voice broke, tears running down her cheeks.

Wes pulled her onto his lap and kissed her. A kiss that started off tender and sweet. Two people comforting one another over their loss and grief. It slowly heated up. Her kiss became hungrier. His hands searched her familiar curves. Her firm, taut breasts filled his hands.

His tongue danced with hers, the temperature between them rising. He'd missed the feel of her. The taste of her warm, sweet skin. He wanted to lose himself in the comfort of their intense passion. But not before he'd told her everything.

He pulled his mouth from hers, their eyes meeting. "There's something you need to know."

Bree stared at him, her chest heaving, her face filled with apprehension. "All right."

"I love you, Bree. And I'm not just telling you that because you said it first. I'm saying it because it's true. I've waited my entire life to feel like this about someone. I've been miserable without you. I'm afraid I was an awful best man during Liam's stag weekend."

Bree grinned.

"What's so funny?"

"I've been miserable without you, too."

Wesley closed the vent on the grill and locked the patio door. He took Bree upstairs and made love to her, in the fullest sense of the words.

Dinner would have to wait.

Chapter 22

Brianna smoothed down the hem of her skirt, her heart beating rapidly. "Are you sure you want to do this tonight?"

Wesley squeezed her hand and grinned. "The way I see it, this is long overdue."

He pressed a warm, lingering kiss to her lips, one strong hand cradling her face.

Bree leaned into his touch and angled her head, allowing Wes to deepen the kiss. His tongue slid between her lips and glided along hers. He released her hand and planted his on the small of her back, pulling her in tighter against him.

She should pull away. Show a little self-control. After all, though they'd declared their love to each other, they'd yet to tell their family and friends.

Kissing openly outside the resort wasn't very discreet. Still, she couldn't pull herself away, reluctant to allow a single inch of space to separate her from the man she loved madly.

They'd spent the majority of their first three days as a bona fide couple in Wesley's bed. Talking, eating, making love. Taking small steps toward planning for a future together.

The prospect of slowly building a life together was exhilarating and terrifying. And she couldn't think of anything that would challenge her more or make her happier.

Wes pulled his mouth from hers reluctantly and groaned. "We'd better not be late. Liam will never let me hear the end of it."

They rounded the corner and entered the pathway that led to the outdoor patio where Liam and Maya's rehearsal dinner was being held. They were greeted by teasing woots and loud kissing noises.

Bree pressed a hand to her open mouth, her cheeks stinging with heat.

"Guess the secret's out." Wes squeezed her hand.

"No matter. It was just about the worst kept secret in the history of secrets." Liam met them on the path and grinned. "And I should know a thing or two about clandestine relationships."

Wes grinned. "Well, I'm glad you and Maya aren't a secret anymore. I'm excited for you both, Liam. I know you'll continue to be very happy together."

"I'm thrilled for you, mate." Liam's self-congratulatory smile could light the entire Eastern seaboard. He held his arms open and hugged them both. "I knew you two were absolutely perfect for each other."

"Does this mean you're confessing to being a meddling matchmaker?" One corner of Wesley's mouth curved, as he tried to hold back a smirk.

"Now that it's worked? Absolutely." Liam chuckled. "Now, if my best mate has had his fill of snogging this lovely young lady—for the time being—I say we get on with this rehearsal. I'm quite in a hurry to marry a lovely young lady of my own."

Liam's eyes practically glowed as he looked at Maya Alvarez. The woman he would stand beside on the Pleasure Cove Beach and make his wife in less than twenty-four hours.

A table of children squealed with joy, and everyone laughed.

"Those are Maya's daughters—Sofia and Gabriella. That's Kai—the bride's nephew. That's Madison—the bride's niece. The little one is Liam's niece Emma and that's her older brother, Max." Wesley gave Bree a breakdown of all the children in attendance.

"Bree, I'm so glad you're here." Lena's eyes sparkled as she approached, gathering them both in a hug. "You two belong together. I've known it since the day I met you. Saw the love he had for you in his eyes. Saw the same in yours."

Bree smiled, her eyes misty with tears as she glanced up at Wes. "You're a very wise woman, Ms. Lena. And you've raised a truly wonderful man."

Wes leaned in and gave Bree a quick kiss on the lips before deftly moving her through the group of family and friends.

They congratulated Maya, whom Bree had met at a previous business dinner. Wes introduced her to the matron-of-honor, Kendra, and her husband Nathan Johnston, a pro football player. Next, he introduced her to Kendra's and Maya's brother Dash Williams and his fiancée Mikayla.

She met a variety of additional relatives. Liam's father, Nigel, and Mrs. Hanson—the woman who had been Liam and Hunter's nanny since they were boys, but now seemed to enjoy a much more personal relationship with their father. The groom's brother, Hunter, and his wife, Meredith. Kendra and Dash's mother, Ms. Anna. The Johnston family, comprised of Nate's parents and several of his siblings, including his fraternal twin sister Vi. Maya's parents—Curtis and Alita Williams, and her brother Cole.

The rehearsal was lovely. Filled with laughter and tears of joy. During the delicious meal that followed, there was more of the same.

Bree felt at home, like she was among family and old friends. She'd been nervous about the prospect of uprooting her life and moving to Pleasure Cove so that she and Wes could be together and close to his mother. But there was so much love, friendship and good-natured teasing here. And they'd gone out of their way to make her feel like she was part of their extended family.

At the end of the night, she and Wes said their goodbyes, saw Lena to her room at the resort, and strolled along the beach hand-in-hand.

London would always be special for them. It was the place where they'd first met and where they'd both realized they'd fallen in love. But here on the sandy beaches of Pleasure Cove among friends who were already beginning to feel like family...this somehow felt like home.

Not his home or her home, but *theirs*. The place where they could make a life together.

Epilogue

Wes was head over heels in love with the girl who was in his arms. She'd stolen his heart in a way he hadn't thought possible.

He wanted to give her the entire world wrapped in a neat little bow. He'd do anything for her.

The edge of her mouth curled as she slept, mimicking a smile. She seemed to know instinctually that she was safe in his arms. That he'd do everything in his power to protect her and provide for her.

He stroked her soft, downy hair and kissed her forehead.

"Mackenzie Alena Adams," he whispered softly. His lips brushed her warm skin as he inhaled her scent. "Do you have any idea how much you mean to me?"

Mackenzie yawned and stretched, her dark eyes opening for a moment before she closed them again and pressed her fist to her lips in a failed attempt to suck it.

"Hungry again, baby girl?" Wes secured the blanket around his daughter, only a few hours old.

Bree grinned as she stroked their daughter's cheek. "She's beautiful, Wes."

"Just like her mama." Wes pressed a soft, lingering kiss to Bree's lips.

He sat on the edge of Bree's bed and wrapped an arm around her as he cradled their daughter in his arms.

They'd been together for two years and were already engaged when Bree had shown him the positive pregnancy test. With the help of their family and friends, they'd managed to coordinate a simple, but elegant ceremony on Pleasure Cove Beach. The same place they'd witnessed Maya and Liam taking their vows two years earlier. They'd both stood barefoot in the sand, the soft sea air rustling her hair, and declared their commitment to each other.

Even now, he got choked up thinking of how beautiful she'd been in her wedding dress. A sleeveless, cream-colored ball gown with a sweetheart neckline that showcased her breasts, enlarged by the pregnancy.

Wes hadn't thought he could be any happier than he was the day Bree stood there on that beach in front of the world and agreed to be his wife.

He'd been wrong.

Witnessing the birth of their daughter had been even more touching, eliciting tears from both of them.

As a husband and a father, his life had taken on new meaning. Bree had given him the life he'd convinced himself he hadn't wanted. Yet he was happier than he ever imagined possible.

"Would you like to hold your baby sister?" Wes beamed at the handsome boy who was nearly fifteen with a face that looked so much like his own.

The boy who'd washed his hands and had been waiting patiently bobbed his head and took the newborn in his arms.

Wesley's heart felt as if it would burst. *His son.* It still didn't feel real. But Bree had made it happen. She'd written letters to Gray's adoptive parents for more than a year before she'd finally gotten a response.

Gray had learned he was adopted and he wanted to meet his biological parents. He'd been angry with Wes at first, but they'd slowly built a relationship over the past year. And four months ago, Gray had finally met his biological mother—Janine.

Wes had been nervous to see her again. He was uncertain of how he'd react to the woman who'd given away their son without telling him. But when he'd laid eyes on Janine and seen the pain and fear on her face, they both had tears of regret in their eyes.

He and Bree had sat and talked with Janine for an hour before Gray arrived with his adoptive parents. And when they parted ways, he managed to hug his son's mother and wish her well. Something that was only possible because of the love and grace he'd learned from his mother and from being with Bree.

They'd been through a lot. Marriage, a growing family and the expansion of two successful businesses. Bree had become a vocal activist for organizations that raised money to battle his mother's illness and those that protected women from boyfriends and exes like

Alex Hunt—whom they hadn't heard from since Bree filed a restraining order against him.

A wide smile spread across Gray's face. "I think she just smiled at me in her sleep."

"She knows she's safe. That her big brother will always be there to protect her." Bree wore a white-and-green hospital gown with a crusty, baby-puke stain on one shoulder. Her curls were secured in a messy topknot.

She looked happy, but exhausted. Still, she was the most beautiful woman he'd ever seen.

The love of his life.

Maybe he didn't deserve Bree, the kids, or the life they were building together, but he was damn grateful for it. And he'd never, ever let any of them go.

* * * * *

COMING NEXT MONTH
Available January 16, 2018

#557 HER UNEXPECTED VALENTINE
Bare Sophistication • by Sherelle Green

Nicole LeBlanc lands a coveted gig as lead makeup artist and hairstylist on a series of Valentine's Day commercials. Once she meets the creative director, she's certain he could fulfill her romantic fantasies. Nicole tempts Kendrick Burrstone to take another chance at love…until a media frenzy jeopardizes it all.

#558 BE MY FOREVER BRIDE
The Kingsleys of Texas • by Martha Kennerson

It was like a fairy tale: eloping with Houston oil tycoon Brice Kingsley. Then a devastating diagnosis and a threat from her past forced Brooke Smith Kingsley to leave. Now she can make things right, but only if she can keep her secret—and her distance—from her irresistible husband.

#559 ON-AIR PASSION
The Clarks of Atlanta • by Lindsay Evans

Ahmed Clark left sports to become a radio show host—one who's cynical about romance. But when Elle Marshall goes on air to promote her business, they clash and sizzle over the airwaves. Putting his heart in play is his riskiest move, but it's the only way to win hers…

#560 A TASTE OF DESIRE
Deliciously Dechamps • by Chloe Blake

International real estate agent Nicole Parks isn't expecting romance in Brazil, but she's falling for French vintner Destin Dechamps. Yet he's out to sabotage the deal that will guarantee her a promotion and the adoption she's been longing for. With their dreams in the balance, is there room for love?

Get 2 Free Books,
Plus 2 Free Gifts—
just for trying the
Reader Service!

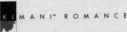

SPECIAL EXCERPT FROM

It was like something out of a fairy tale: being swept off her feet, then eloping with her one true love, Houston oil tycoon Brice Kingsley. Then a devastating diagnosis and a threat from her past forced Brooke Smith Kingsley to leave the man she loved. Now she has a chance to make things right, but only if she can keep her secret—and her distance—from her irresistible husband.

Read on for a sneak peek at
BE MY FOREVER BRIDE, the next exciting
installment in author Martha Kennerson's
***THE KINGSLEYS OF TEXAS** series!*

Brooke opened the door and walked into the office to find Brice seated behind his desk, signing several documents. "Did you forget something, Amy?"

The sound of his voice sent waves of desire throughout her body, just like they had from the first moment they met. She'd missed it… She'd missed him. "It's not Amy, Brice," Brooke replied, closing the door behind her, knowing this conversation wasn't for the public.

Brice dropped his pen, raised his head and sat back in his seat. "Brooke," he said, his face expressionless.

"Do you have a moment for a quick chat?" She tried to project confidence when in reality she was a nervous wreck inside. Her heart was beating so fast she just knew the whole building could hear it.

Brice tilted his head slightly to the right and his forehead crinkled. "You tell me after six months of what I thought was a wonderful marriage that you want out. I convince you to give us time to work things out—at least I thought I had—and go out for your favorite seafood only to come back to find that you've left me with a note." He leaned forward slightly. "You disappear for three months, only communicating through your lawyer, and now you want to chat." His tone was hard but even.

"I…I—"

"Sure, please have a seat." His words were laced with disdain and sarcasm.

Brooke moved forward on unsteady legs, reaching for the support of a chair. She swallowed hard. "You make it sound so—"

"So what? Honest? Is that not what happened?"

"I didn't want to fight. Not then and certainly not now," she explained, trying to hold his angry glare.

"What *do* you want, Brooke?" Brice asked, sitting back in his chair.

"It's simple. I'd like to get through these next several weeks as painlessly as possible. We're both professionals with a job to do."

Brice sat up in his chair. "That we are." He reached into his desk drawer and pulled out a manila envelope. "We can start by you signing the settlement papers so the lawyers can move forward with the divorce."

Don't miss BE MY FOREVER BRIDE
by Martha Kennerson, available February 2018
wherever Harlequin® Kimani Romance™
books and ebooks are sold!

KPEXP0118

Want to give in to temptation with steamy tales of irresistible desire?

Check out **Harlequin® Presents®**, **Harlequin® Desire** and **Harlequin® Kimani™ Romance** books!

New books available every month!

CONNECT WITH US AT:

Harlequin.com/Community

 Facebook.com/HarlequinBooks

 Twitter.com/HarlequinBooks

 Instagram.com/HarlequinBooks

 Pinterest.com/HarlequinBooks

ReaderService.com

**ROMANCE WHEN
YOU NEED IT**

PGENRE2017

LOVE
Harlequin romance?

Join our Harlequin community to share your thoughts and connect with other romance readers!

Be the first to find out about promotions, news, and exclusive content!

Sign up for the Harlequin e-newsletter and download a free book from any series at **www.TryHarlequin.com**

CONNECT WITH US AT:

Harlequin.com/Community

 Facebook.com/HarlequinBooks

 Twitter.com/HarlequinBooks

 Instagram.com/HarlequinBooks

 Pinterest.com/HarlequinBooks

ReaderService.com

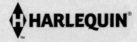 **HARLEQUIN**®

ROMANCE WHEN YOU NEED IT